The Man adjusted the wide brim of his hat and lit his cigarette. The sun rose slowly in the sky, already baking the dry grassland around him. Exhaling grey-blue smoke, he stooped and hefted the satchel containing his precious cargo, his hydraulic lifters hissing gently from the plate on his back.

He pressed a button on the side of his visor and examined the horizon from the crest of the hill. Behind him was a seaside town, its name lost in history. He needed to go East, and North. His gaze fell on a small town up ahead, probably also nameless. He nodded slightly to himself, and walked. He always walked. It was what he did.

The wind rushed through the town's gate as Walker entered. Dust swirled and danced at his feet as he stepped down the main street. He vaguely recognised it as one he had visited before on his rounds, but its name eluded him for the moment. It was typical of most small English towns; wide main road, flanked by concrete pedestrian areas. Of course, only the Order drove vehicles these days, and they rarely ventured this far out; the people wandered about freely.

He double checked the bindings on his satchel; he couldn't afford to have any of its contents stolen from him, before checking his pistol holster. As he walked down the dilapidated main street, with its old brickwork buildings shored up with timber, he thumbed some tobacco from the pocket on the pack at his hip and rolled himself another cigarette.

The township was quiet, as always this early in the day, but the market-men were already set up, lounging in their lean-to stalls against the larger buildings lining the street. As Walker paced through he occasionally glanced around at their wares, showing interest in the stalls with the rarer mechanical objects, or those with more exotic looking items. He approached one stall. A hairy beast of a man sat behind it, sweating profusely in the bitter autumn heat. The man was fanning himself, and looked sourly up at Walker as he examined the items on the desk.

"'Ere, don't break anything, matey" The merchant warned. He jerked his thumb lazily towards a burly man, bald head covered in tattoos, who was standing to the right of the stall."Mr Edwards can get a bit, hah, emotional, especially in this morning heat"

He allowed himself a humourless smile, all yellowing teeth and venom. Walker nodded slightly and continued to browse the rubbish on the stall in front of him. He clucked to himself; from afar it had appeared interesting, but he saw that it was mainly junk; discarded old world items, shabby and aged electronic gadgets that served little purpose when they were new, and much less now that they had stopped working.

1

He picked up a flat plastic device, about the same size as a book, but much thinner. He turned it this way and that, watching as the sun gleamed from one of its flat edges. He supposed it had been a device similar in function to those used in the city, albeit a much uglier, heavier piece of rubbish. Walker could hear the merchant grumbling more about 'damaging the goods' and 'damned tourists'.

He glanced at the merchant. The man was still desperately trying to stop the flow of sweat by waving at himself with a strip cardboard; his red and green striped tunic was drenched and stained. Walker put the dead tablet down, nodded his thanks to Edwards and flipped a copper penny to the merchant. As the merchant bit the coin, supposedly to test its purity, Walker walked on, ignoring the growls about timewasters and moved on into the market.

It was just before noon and the township had come alive. Children ran and played in the dusty street as merchants bellowed and cried about prices and stocks. People milled; some with obvious business and some with nothing to do but mill and bake in the sun. Local militia men patrolled the streets, sweating in their mismatched armour and scowling at innocent and guilty people alike, pretending to keep some semblance of order.

Walker ambled through the crowd, which parted easily around him. Out here, in these backwater towns, people knew to give a wide berth to anyone who looked even remotely of the Order; people remembered what the Order was capable of. He didn't mind; he quite enjoyed the feeling of power it brought. He smiled slightly to himself.

He would continue to search the market for any clues, but knew it would be in vain. It was a rare thing indeed to find any of his chosen wares in small town markets such as this one. Walker sighed and stopped in the middle of the busy street. As usual the crowd, with some low muttering again about tourists, parted around him. He gazed down the street and saw a pub. He began to stroll down the street again, his hydraulic mounted boots clinking gently with every step, the sound lost in the bustle of the crowd.

He reached the tavern and flicked his cigarette stub away, bending low through the doorway. It took a moment for his eyes to adjust to the smoky darkness after the blazing morning sun from outside, and in that moment everything in the bar stopped. He wrinkled his nose slightly at the smell, and gazed around the dimly lit bar. A seating area was to his left, where the front of the bar was located. The bar itself was shaped like a backwards L and continued down the musty narrow room, where Walker could make out more seats and what he presumed to be a back entrance.

He glanced around, noting anyone who might cause trouble, as well as checking for potential contacts. Walker couldn't help but chuckle; even at this relatively early hour, the pub was fairly full, a relic of English tradition. Aside from the usual bar flies and wastrels, there were three people that caught his eye. A red faced, balding man, one eyed and scarred, sitting at the bar facing the doorway. The others were to Walker's left; one was lanky like a beanpole with a little potbelly, pale and ill looking in the shabby light, ogling in

Walker's direction. He would have gone unnoticed if not for his drinking partner, who had stiffened when he had walked in.

She was younger than her partner; not yet a woman grown by the looks of it, but it was hard to tell. Her eyes were hidden behind a half visor, similar to Walker's, which began at the top of the forehead and went around the head and down to where it rested on the nose, but he could practically feel the stare she was directing his way.

He rubbed his chin at that; the visors were normally issued only by authorities, normally the Order. She was scowling, her lips a sharp slash of displeasure. Walker noted their positions and strode to the bar.

"Whiskey. Neat" he muttered.

The bartender, a sallow faced woman of indeterminate age, nodded bleakly and lifted a flagon from under the bar. As she went to pour, Walker shook his head and spoke softly, "Not that one. The good stuff, please"

The woman clucked her disapproval, like a hen, but grabbed a small stool from under the bar. With it, she reached up into a small cupboard, located above the bar itself, and fetched an aging brown bottle. She un-bunged the cork, and got Walker a less than fresh glass. She poured him a shot. Walker held up two fingers. She poured again, stopped the bottle back up and pushed the glass over towards Walker. He nodded his thanks and sipped at the drink, enjoying the oaky taste as the warmth slipped down the back of his throat, resting in his stomach.

"'Ow you gunna pay then, eh?" She spoke with the resurgent, brackish West-Country twang.

Walker took another sip, as the woman continued to worry.

"That stuff's expensive my luv, but I'm sure a strappin' walker loike youm got a few goodies in that bag o' yers?"

She eyed the satchel at Walker's hip greedily; he couldn't help notice her eyes dart, however briefly, toward the small scarred man sat around the corner of the bar.

Walker smiled easily and slowly finished the drink, "Now, I'm just here for some information. We can do business."

He looked expansively around the room. The couple he had noticed earlier were both watching him; the beanpole gawping vacantly, the teen staring intently. He corrected himself mentally; he couldn't know for sure what she was thinking, behind that half-mask lens the eyes were invisible. He saw no trouble in the room, aside from old red face.

"I have money, of course. Amongst other things."

He patted his satchel, felt the books and papers inside, the solidness of the heavy volumes; knew he had to use them wisely. The bald man with the scar spoke up; gravel voiced and too many drinks in.

"Books, walker man? You think we want books?" He spat.

It was red face; broken and blistered veins spread across his nose, black and blue from the years of drinking. He was wearing a tattered jacket, emblazoned with the eagle skull of some old military unit; his arms were heavily tattooed but faded with age. His left eye was a vile jaundice yellow, bloodshot; his right a grey, milky tone that immediately suggested blindness. The scar, trailing from the back of his head and through his face, bisecting the eye, only enforced this. He was a veteran, clearly.

They drank cheaply, but had little to do. Anger, pain and hard, dangerous governmental training made these individuals resentful, bored and dangerous. Walker turned his gaze towards him, eyes hidden behind the impervious sheen of his half-mask visor. He slowly rolled a cigarette, letting the veteran's anger build. The cigarette bloomed red briefly in the gloom of the pub as Walker struck his match. He breathed deep and let out a plume of blue-grey smoke.

He carefully kept his voice accent-free, to build on their already palpable hatred, "I'm assuming you can't read?"

The man bristled, but Walker carried on, "That doesn't mean you're stupid though. You know books are valuable. Everyone knows it."

The veteran scowled at him over his pint glass. "We don't need books round here. Guns, food, money, workin' for a livin'. S'wat it's all about. Readin' gets folk killed, brings about the guvverment types."

He looked about, meaningfully. There were a few mutters of agreement, but clearly not the support the veteran had expected from his fellow bar folk.

Walker continued to stare at him, as the old man glared around at the other patrons, before turning to the landlady, "Do you even know how to read, Bernie?"

She glared at him, "What a question to arsk a lady, eh? Course I does". She waved dismissively at him and turned back to Walker, "I just aint got the time. 'Ere then, what's in that ole satchel o' yours? Got anythin' good?"

Walker stopped staring at the man and turned back to the barmaid. "Depends what you want, m'dear. Why don't we look and see?"

The veteran snorted. "Damn all this readin' bollocks."

He drained his pint and stood up abruptly, knocking his stool over. He limped from the bar, grumbling and staring at Walker with acid hatred plastered across his face. Walker tipped his hat to him as he went past and turned back to Bernie as the door slammed behind him. He allowed himself a sidelong glance to where bean pole and the girl had been sat, but they had left while he had been distracted by the veteran.

Walker scowled inwardly. He had a feeling that he had missed something. He would have to try and quash this uneasiness while he plied his trade. He spread his arms expansively and, speaking louder, addressed the whole bar.

4

Ten Years ago...

The girl stood on the steps, holding her mother's hand. The shiny faced men who hid their real faces had come and ransacked the house, taking all the books, papers and notes her parents had managed to collect. He lay across the front porch, huddled and cowed, face held to stop the bleeding of his nose. His shotgun lay next to him, still smoking from the pot shots he had taken at the big metal cart. He wasn't moving much and was lucky the men hadn't just shot him back. She knew better than to move to help him.

The men who hid their faces had hit her brother too, because he was bigger than her and had tried to help her father. The men had a boss, who only half hid his face. His eyes were hidden behind shiny, dark glass and his face was pointy, long beak like nose crowning a sad looking mouth. He was tall, taller than her father, but thinner. He was like a big bird, she thought, one of the ones who ate dead things. He had the same hunched shoulders and a flapping cape like wings; she could almost see him spreading the heavy, tattered leather and flying off, her father in his clutches to feed his ugly bird-children.

As she watched the no –faced men 'teaching' her brother, she looked up at her mother. She looked sad, but the girl wasn't sure what she was sad about. Was she sad for her father, coughing in the dirt? Or for the treasures the men were taking away from them?

Her mother and father had explained why it was important to hide the treasures from these men, said it was important to 'preserve knowledge', but the girl hadn't known what they meant. She did know hiding the books was pointless though. Everyone got caught around here. Their neighbour, the nice old lady who had always smiled and waved in the mornings, had been taken away for a while by other no-face men. When they brought her back, she had stopped smiling. She stood watching through the cracked windows of her home over the road, expressionless and still. Everyone got caught. Everyone except the Walkers.

The bird man had stooped to say something to her father, still lying in the dust in front of their house. The girl had no idea what he could be saying, but she supposed it didn't matter; more warnings about learning, more of the same that she had heard all of her life. The bird man straightened up and glanced at the two of them stood on the concrete steps leading to her house. He simply looked on, doing nothing.

She suddenly wished she could see his eyes, but they were still hidden behind the dark glass. He said something in a soft voice that didn't quite carry over the winds that blew through their town, and the lesson was over. One of them lugged a sack full of the treasures her parents had safeguarded and they made their way to the metal cart still waiting.

As the vehicle roared into life, sputtering thick clouds of oily smoke, her mother let out a sob and ran to her father, clutching his head and mopping the blood from his nose and chin. The girl slowly walked to where her brother sat nursing his gut, where the shiny faced men had left him winded.

"I told you" she said quietly, holding her hand out to help him up. "I told you they'd come. It's the rules. That's what they say".

Her brother spat and stood shakily, ignoring her outstretched hand. "I know what you told me" he gasped, resting his hands on his knees to catch his breath. "But you know we gotta protect it. It's important, like Mum and Dad said. How can you not care?"

He glared down at her, squinting through his tears. She sighed and wondered how her older brother couldn't see it. She did care, she cared a lot. She cared for her father, strong and dependable, full of his morals and lessons. She cared for her mother, clever and quick, who knew lots about the world outside of the village. She cared for her brother, smiling and tall, like her father, but sillier. She cared about her neighbour, who never smiled. And she cared for books, and for words. The man had known better ways of doing this, she was sure.

He had strolled into the town slowly, almost nonchalantly, smoking too many cigarettes and smiling, as if everything was funny. He wore a wide brimmed hat, like in old timey pictures. At his side was a large sack, tied off securely at the top, and he carried a large gun, holstered to his leg.

Guns meant trouble, and most of the town had stayed inside and watched from behind threadbare curtains as the stranger wandered through town. Only the girl had braved the winds outside and gone to speak to the stranger. She remembered his smell; unwashed body odour and cigarette smoke.

She remembered his voice, too, which was deep and almost painfully slow, as if he weighed each word up, valuing it, before using it. She couldn't remember what they actually spoke about, but she had offered to take him around the town for ten pence. He had laughed at her cheek, but had agreed, flicking the coin into her open palms.

They chattered as they rambled around the concrete town, occasionally stopping at shops or taverns. At every business that was closed, she would ask what he was looking for, and every time he would ignore her. At every open shop or pub, he would go in and speak quietly, and she would be made to stay outside; every time he came out he would check the untidy bag hanging from his shoulder.

She remembered now how he had avoided the town's militia, ducking aside or pulling his hat lower over his face.

After nearly a day of walking and touring all of the shops and bars she could think of, they had stopped.

The walker had patted her on the head, thanked her, and had started to walk out of the town, when the girl had called to him, "Hey! Mister! You never told me what you were looking for! Did you find it? It was treasure, wasn't it? You were looking for treasure."

The man had chuckled, walked back to her and knelt down in the dust, his cloak flapping lightly in the wind. Their faces were level, but she could only see her own wide, slightly frightened eyes reflected in his half visor, which was silvery but still not see through.

"What treasure do you mean, girl?"

The girl swallowed, he was more imposing up close; he still smiled, but there was something else there... something hidden away. His stubble seemed rougher and darker and his smell was so strong it seemed to push her backwards on her heels.

"Not shiny treasure, like in stories. Real treasure"

It had seemed that they were still then for an age, his eyeless visor shining in her face, her staring into her own reflection. Even the wind had seemed to die down, to listen to what the walker would say.

She had flinched when the man abruptly reached into the sack at his hip. He held something out to her. She looked slowly down at a book. It was old, cracked and peeling; words had once been delicately printed on its surface, but all that remained were the letters TRE; the rest of the cover was torn. She had stared, entranced.

She had nearly missed him speaking, "How old are you, girl?"

She hadn't looked up when she replied, "I'm ten. Ten and a bit... Is this for me? I never had a book before. Are you a walker? My dad told me some stuff about walkers."

In fact, she realised, looking over at her father in the dust, sitting up now and muttering at her mother to fetch some cider, that her father had told her a lot about these walker men, with their guns and books.

They had been a kind of soldier, he said. Felosophers, her Dad had called them. Felosophers were a kind of old soldier, he had said, that went around looking after books. He had spoken about something called the Order, and how walkers and felosophers were once the same, but she had gotten confused. Her mother had refused to explain until she was older. She thought it was too horrible.

She had never met a walker before, until that one had arrived and given her a book of her own, a book still hidden behind one of the loose bricks in the old, orange building marked W/C on the edge of town: the book about adventures and exciting men, with wooden 'ships' that swam the ocean, searching for treasure in faraway lands. But the men in this book weren't looking for real treasure, not like the walker that had come through town.

As her brother stood watching the no-eyed men's driving machine disappear over the horizon, and her father sat shaking with his mug of cider, she remembered what the walker had said to her, after he had asked how old she was.

"Keep this safe, girl, and show it to me if we meet again. Remember; knowledge is better than strength. Learn how to read, but not just books, people too. Learn all you can, and about all you can, from who you can. Keeping books in one place doesn't help. What I do, that's all that works. These," he indicated the book in her hand, "Are the key to everything. Knowledge is power, girl. Remember that."

He had left her then, without another word, and walked out of the town, not looking back.

3

Walker left the bar and scowled. The bar flies had managed to trick him out of two books, not one; a cookbook he had used regularly in his travels, and an ancient story book about a version of Earth that was flat and magical. Disc something.

He rolled himself a cigarette and re-checked the straps on his satchel. He had left the tavern with nothing aside from a sour mood. He leaned under the shade of a stall, much to the merchant's chagrin, and surveyed the town. He was annoyed, not just at the illiterate locals who would surely be abusing his gifts and using the pages to wipe their arses within a week, but at himself for not being able to talk his way out of it. He had been distracted; that teen in the corner, with the man... his thoughts trailed off, roiling darkly like autumn storm clouds.

He sighed and strode away from the bar and the stall, out into the afternoon sun and the concrete streets of the town. He kept his head down and tried to look unbothered, knowing that he was being followed. The teen and her male friend were on the rooftops to his left, trying unsuccessfully to shadow him, themselves casting long shadows on the street next to him.

Walker turned right and slipped nimbly down one of the many rubbish strewn alleys of the town.

The teen swore.

"He's gone," she muttered to her partner. He was puffing gently, sweat running down his soft face.

"Come on, you don't actually think it's the same guy, do you? It's just another walker; they all stink of shit and think they're better than us." He flopped down on a defunct and rusted air-conditioning unit and closed his eyes against the sun.

The teen rolled her eyes and looked away from her brother. The years had not been kind to him; since their father's death, he'd stopped caring. Drink and easy drugs had softened his once strong body, leaving a man that looked and acted many years older than his true age.

She retracted her half visor and tried to peer into the alley that the walker had vanished into, but could only see shadows and litter whipped up by the winds. She crouched and ran her fingers through her dark hair, trying to stop it from blowing into her eyes. She had been waiting ten years for this, ten years for something to happen. But she had missed her chance, he had been there, in Bernie's bar but her cowardly brother had stopped her from confronting him.

"Anyway, he looks pretty dangerous. Even if it was the guy who gave you that book, suppose he didn't remember you? It's too hot up here." Her brother sighed and scratched his arm. "I need some Flash, I'm tired."

He stood, slowly, and stretched his back. She heard the clicks and pops as he momentarily stood straight, before he resumed his usual hunch. "Come on," He began, "We can still catch..." He broke off slowly, as something clicked menacingly.

The walker was there, holding his handgun against her brother's forehead.

Her stomach dropped away in fear, but her eyes widened in anticipation, "It's—" He cut her off.

"Why are you following me?" He growled. A cigarette hung lazily from his mouth, moving as his words rumbled out, threatening to drop but never quite managing it.

She gulped. "It's... it's me" she murmured. She clenched her fists, squashing her anxiety. Her brother shook, eyes closed, mouthing some prayer that no god would hear.

Her words fought each other, tumbling out in her excitement, "You gave me the book!

"We were following you to make sure it was you, but I know it's you, you haven't changed a bit; you even smell the same," she caught the gushing tone of her voice, and added, "Don't you ever wash?"

She could feel the walker's gaze from under his visor, the same one she had seen her own reflection in all those years ago. The cigarette moved from one side of his mouth to the other, and then suddenly, he laughed. It was a soft one, and didn't last long, but it seemed genuine.

He rubbed his chin and murmured, "Treasure Island girl". He lowered the gun, and made a show of patting off her brother's sleeve.

"Sorry there fella," The man said, as he replaced his weapon. "Can't be too careful around these parts. Some people don't care for walkers these days."

She opened her mouth to speak, but he turned and, with two long strides, was face to face with her. It suddenly dawned on her how much taller than her he was; even now she had grown taller herself. His smell was just as pungent, his chin still stubbled and unkempt.

"Takes guts to offend a man's smell when he's just had a gun pointed at her fella's head." He grinned, "Been a while."

He offered her his hand, but she ignored him. "Firstly" her brow furrowed slightly, "He's my brother, not my 'fella'. Secondly," she roughly pushed his outstretched hand away, "Where the hell have you been? I've been waiting ten years for you to show up!"

She turned to her brother, who had collapsed onto the gravelly rooftop, holding his chest. "I told you it was him. One of the ones Dad used to tell us about. He gave me that book" She turned back to Walker. "The walker. And you led the no-eyed men here."

She resumed her scowl, glaring into the eyeless, grinning face under the vintage cowboy hat.

Walker's grin faded. No-eyed men were what uneducated townsfolk called the helmeted government agents, subordinate to the philosophers, unofficially known as the Bookmen. He scratched his chin and stepped back from the girl. It was indeed the same one he met on one of his early excursions out west; this was why the town felt familiar to him. The town been raided shortly after he had visited; not unusual, really.

"So?" He grunted.

She rubbed at her eye and spoke. "The government men came, a few weeks after you did. They asked my dad about you, after they beat him. He lasted a little longer after that. They...." She looked away, out over the rooftops.

Walker sighed.

The girl turned back to him. "My Dad told me about you, about the order of felosophers, and walkers." She ran her hand through her hair, and pressed on. "Which one are you? A felosopher or a walker?"

He flinched at the mispronunciation of his word, but shot her a smile, "Does it matter?"

She eyed him up for a second, then shrugged. She took a tattered book from her hip pouch, the scored leather cover dull in the sunlight, pausing to run a fond finger down its battered spine. She held the book out to him. "Here it is. *Treasure Island*. I've read it a thousand times, or more, like you said."

She smiled up at him, "I remember what you said as well, that I should find you, when I'm ready? Well, I am, and I'm here. I'm ready to go with you."

Walker stared at her grimly. The girl was mad, clearly; he couldn't even remember why he told her those things in the first place. "Why do you want to come with me, girl?"

She opened her mouth to speak, but he interrupted.

"And why do you think I'd let you?"

She gawped at him, *Treasure Island* limp in her outstretched hand, "But, you said... You gave me the book. I was supposed to go with—"

He cut in, "I don't need you, girl. I especially don't need *him*." He jerked a thumb towards her brother, who was still lying on in the gravel on the roof.

She stood there, mouth open. "But... you said. You said to find you. I've been waiting, getting ready! Training, learning to read, everything you said".

He ignored her pleas, "No".

He saw the big, sad eyes he had seen when she was a youth, red rimmed and glistening in the afternoon sun. They glared accusingly at him.

"You can't do this... You're one of them, right? A felosopher? You're supposed to help people."

Walker gritted his teeth. "Say it right" he growled.

She stood there, uncomprehending "What?"

"It's Philosopher. P-h-i-l-o-s-o-p-h-e-r." He spelled it out. "No E at the beginning." Walker turned and started to stalk back to the ladder that had taken him to the roof.

He heard a metal crunch, and knew she had a gun pointed at him. Home-made, by the sound the round had made on its way into the chamber.

"You'd better take the shot. It's the only one you'll get"

Walker turned slowly towards her, arms loosely held at his sides. The girl was holding out a cobbled together 'hand cannon'. The magnum round was enough to puncture his rusty, aging chest armour, but he wasn't about to let her know that. He started to step slowly towards her. The girl's arm shook, but she continued to hold the gun up at chest level.

"You... you can't go around, doing what you do, getting people hurt" The girl's voice was emotional. She wiped at her eyes again. "You just mince around from place to place, not caring; taking what you want, doing what you want, getting people killed. It's... it's not fair".

Walker shook his head and took another step towards her. "You really don't know who we are, do you?" He asked her.

The gun in her grasp started to waver. He reached out slowly and took it from her. Her brother was still sitting, staring open mouthed at the two of them. The girl's shoulders slumped, and she sniffed.

"I thought you were here to change things. Take me away from this. My Dad said you were supposed to be good. That walkers and felosophers helped people." She paused to glare up at him, "Sorry, the P-h-i-l-o-s-o-p-h-e-r-s" She spelled it out slowly, as if to a child, as he had to her.

Walker sighed, and stepped back, lightly holding her pistol. The girl stood there, scowling, fists clenched. "Do you know what the difference is?"

"Difference? My Dad didn't tell me about differences." she replied quietly. "He told me about the Order, and about philosophers, about how the Walkers aren't the same but kind of are, how they go about saving books, giving them back to people. The Order Philosophers just gather them up and store them away."

Walker nodded to himself and dropped the pistol to the ground. "You know little, girl, and that's fine by me. Keep your dreams to yourself, and keep me out of them."

She ignored the gun and stepped forward. "Walker, wait." She went to grab his arm, but stopped as he glanced down. She carried on hastily. "Take me with you. I did as you said. I'm ready to look after the treasure, the books. I'm ready to join, to do my bit."

Walker snorted derisively. "You want to join the Walkers? You don't even know who we are, what we do. And this?" He kicked the ramshackle gun towards her, "Doesn't make you ready." He pointed to the beanpole, who had sat staring, doing nothing, "And he certainly isn't."

He sneered at the two of them, "If you had learned like I told you, you'd know this is impossible. You can't just waltz up and join."

"There was no one to learn from. I expected you back, sooner. But you never came."

Walker shrugged, "I doubt you'll find anyone who cares, girl. I never have."

It was her turn to sneer. "Is that why you're out here, alone?" She asked spitefully.

Walker's mouth turned hard, frosty. "I don't need you," he said, deadpan, "Go home."

"Wait! Hey! Where are you going? I need to..." she trailed off, as Walker walked away.

He left them on the rooftop, her staring numbly and her brother pale, slumped against a rusting reminder of the past.

6

Walker glowered furiously. The cheek of it. Little girls had no business with the Walkers. He climbed down the ladder from the roof leaving her watching him.

He should have known better than to get involved with the common folk out here, to repeat the mistakes of the past. She was too young, callow and untrained. He couldn't risk getting involved; Walker didn't do babysitting.

It was as he dismounted the ladder, thoughts racing through his mind, preoccupying him, that his distractions betrayed him for the second time that day.

A blinding pain screamed up his spine and winded him utterly. He collapsed backwards, knocking dustbins and rubbish askew, and, as he slipped into dark unconsciousness, he thought he could make out a bald, scarred head and a single yellow eye, leering from the shade.

As the yellowing sun began to set, casting long, murky shadows, Jim the veteran, limping heavily as he went, dragged his heavy load down towards the bar.

He licked his lips at the thought of the scrumpy ole Bernie would send his way, and heaved the body along some more. The walker groaned, and Jim put the boot in, knocking him out with a swift kick to the jaw. He was a tough sonofabitch, Jim would give him that. Tall too, probably a good head taller'n most, he thought.

The man's armour didn't help Jim's cause none either. He spat a glob of phlegm and paused, stretching his back, savouring the crunch his joints made. It'd been a long time since Jim had seen a lifter rig like the man at his feet was wearing. Military power armour, philosopher rank by the looks of it; none complete too. Jim had seen many in his time. This man was showing his ineptitude; the armour was in embarrassing condition.

He grunted as he began to drag the man again, by the foot, down the alley towards the back of the bar; Bernie would never let him in the front with his haul. Jim opened a door and, after peering into the shadows around him to check that no one had followed, dumped the walker through the opening.

He paused to take a breath and a shot of gunfire from the flask at his hip. As he felt the red burn begin in his belly, he grinned, thinking of the treasure the unconscious walker must have in store for them. He pocketed his flask and headed through the hanging, wooden back door to the bar.

It was evening by the time the girl and her brother got back to the bar. It seemed gloomier than before; the walker had thoroughly ruined the girl's mood, as well as her plans. Her brother had his Flash, and had cheered up noticeably, but she only had the sour bourbon that Bernie put up cheap, and it was doing nothing for her. The bar seemed quieter too; the barmaid was whispering at the back with the veteran, Jim; they both seemed excited about something, and Bernie kept disappearing through the back door marked 'private'.

She sighed and drained her whiskey. She couldn't believe what had happened; walkers were supposed to be good, and kind, helping people stand up to the government Philosophers. The man she had met was none of these things. Selfish bastard.

She looked around and managed to catch Bernie's eye as she flitted in from the back. The woman came forward, eyeing the girl, "Same again, isit my love?"

The girl nodded and the dour woman poured. As she went to leave, the girl's brother piped up from his Flash induced stupor, "Where do you keep disappearin' our Bern'?" he slurred, spraying spittle on alternate letters.

Bernie glared at him, "None of your business young man, peoples what asks questions where they's not wanted can gets in trouble, mark my words!"

She gave the girl a meaningful look and stormed out again, leaving the two of them alone at the bar.

As the girl glowered at her drink, thinking of what to do next, there was a loud crack and a shout from the private door. Bernie and Jim burst back in to the room; Bernie's nose was bleeding and the old soldier was redder than usual.

He was shouting, "We should do 'im now Bern! No one does that to my woman an' gets away wiv it!" He began to pull something from his grubby jeans, but Bernie stopped him, dabbing the blood away with a greasy bar cloth.

"Nod ib da bar, nod ib da bar! People will see" She looked around conspiratorially and stopped her gaze on the girl and her brother, who had passed out again.

The girl swallowed her drink and stood up. "Sounds like you two need a hand. Who've you got back there this time?"

It was unusual for Bernie to start without her; Daisy usually chose the mark. Daisy asked again, "Who is it?"

Bernie piped up from the shadows, "We started without you, dear. You'll unnerstand when you sees him."

Daisy walked around the corner of the bar towards the two of them, leaving her gun and pouch with her brother. The couple looked at each other, then the barmaid took the cloth from her nose and arched an eyebrow sceptically.

"You wants payin' fer this un? Or just gonna take his valuables again?"

Daisy replied, "We'll see what he has first, talk about it after."

Jim chuckled and rubbed at his milky eye," A proper mercenary, this un, an' no mistake."

Bernie dabbed at her nose; the blood had stopped but she was still fretting, "Well, you'll definitely like this un then, my luv, he's a right fancy chap and no mistake"

She gestured that the girl should follow, and headed through the door at the back of the room.
The girl sighed, and followed; she had only taken part in these robberies to earn a meagre living, and to keep herself in the loop.

The man they had robbed last week had turned out to be the wrong man; thin streak of piss, soft, too clean and prissy. The man had ordered something called Whine; she imagined that was why he had been constantly moaning. But he had worn an eye visor, the thing she had been searching for, for signs of the walker. When he had proved to be the wrong man, she had taken it from him in a temper.

She followed Bernie and her partner as they scurried towards the back room, feeling the soft hairs at the base of her neck stiffen, wondering who their newest victim was.

As she stepped through the darkness of the narrow back room, she smelled the rot and dampness; it always surprised her how, despite the heat of the English autumn, the ageing buildings remained so cold and damp.

Slowly, her eyes started to adjust. They were in the small back room, longer than it was wide, smelling of dank rot and uncared for furniture. She could make out a slumped shape secured to a chair at the back of the room. The figure was big, or rather, was quite tall, definitely a man: she could hear his deep breathing; for someone who had been captured he was strangely calm. As she got closer to the man she could make out more details, his chest was large, still, his head... She stopped dead. Even in the gloom she could make out the dull gleam of Walker's visor.

Bernie had gotten to the far wall, next to the imprisoned walker and had turned on the tiny lamp on the ancient, rotting desk behind the chair; it threw the room into stark relief. The girl could see the mould now, not just smell it. Ancient metallic beer kegs lined the left wall; the secret back entrance to the alley was on her right. But she was focused on the walker. He was slumped and bleeding from under his visor. They had taken his bag, along with his pistol and cloak, and put them on the desk behind him, his hat lay forgotten on the floor.

As she came closer he looked up at her and chuckled hoarsely.

16

Everything happened at once. The veteran was quick on the uptake. The old man's smile faded and became a bestial snarl as he lurched towards the girl, his crippled leg giving him strange, animalistic movements. Bernie ran to the desk, reaching for the walker's pistol, still in its holster.

As she fumbled with the strapping, the veteran grabbed for the girl, latching onto her sleeve and pulling her ferociously, "She's wiv him!" he growled, yanking her across the room.

The girl and the veteran tumbled; she kicking and punching with all her might, he trying to get his gnarled hands around her throat. The girl panicked; he was strong for his age, and had been trained well. As his hands found her throat and squeezed she lashed out, desperately trying to stop him choking her. The old man leered down, his single yellow eye too close to hers. She could smell his breath, strong alcohol and old food, and could see the tiny burst veins on his nose and cheeks.

As lights started to pop in her vision, he snarled, "Stay still, m'girl. This won't take long."

He began to laugh, but was cut off; the girl had managed to get a knee free and it had found home. As he wheezed and loosened his grip, she scrambled to her feet and swung him with all her might towards some of the stacked kegs to her left. He crashed into a small pile, knocking the tower over. His bulk was quickly lost in the pile of falling debris.

Bernie screamed; she had still not managed to get the gun from its holster. The girl was panting; she looked to where part of the scarred man's body protruded from the mess of metal. He was not moving and a pool of blood was seeping from under the heap, spreading slowly along the floor.

Bernie screamed again, "You killed 'im! You killed 'im! What did you do that fer?"

Suddenly she was hurtling towards her, waving the holster like a flail; leather straps whipping round her head as she ran.

The girl tensed and dodged; Bernie went storming past, staring wide eyed at the girl. She tripped and fell, bringing yet more kegs falling down around them. The girl managed to leap clear; Bernie was not so lucky. The girl covered her ears against the cacophony of falling metal.

As the dust calmed and the crashing stopped, she could hear something over the sound of her own heavy breathing; a dry, bass rumble. She slowly turned around to face the walker, still in his chair, hands and legs bound, chuckling to himself quietly.

She clutched her chest, struggling to regain her breath and control the adrenaline surging around her body. Her hands shook, she felt like crying, her heart was about to burst free and join her blood with Jim's on the floor. She collapsed onto one of the overturned barrels, holding her head in shaking hands.

"What are you laughing at? You know what this means? I've killed someone! Two people! We can't stay here anymore; people will come looking when they know what happened!" She turned to him, wide eyed, but the walker only laughed harder.

As she glared and spat, he slowly stopped laughing, and grinned at her.

9

Walker rubbed the life back in to his arms; they were numb from the veteran's over-exuberant knot tying. Thankfully, the auto injectors in his boots had kept his feet alive and well during his captivity. He stretched.

The girl was still worrying; she had flicked her visor down and was rubbing the purpling bruise at her throat.

He turned to the desk and examined his book satchel. They hadn't managed to open it, which was good; the new lock mechanism was paying for itself. He brushed some grime from the bag before shouldering it. The hydraulic plate on his back took the strain and he reached for his cloak, fastening it about his neck, under the connector on the front of his chest plate. He turned back towards the girl and motioned with his hand.

"Gun"

The girl simply looked at him, "No 'thank you'? No 'well done'? Just 'gun'?"

Walker chuckled again, "Nope, just gun."

He noticed how her fists clenched and unclenched and he scratched his chin. She stooped to pick his gun, still in its holster, from the ground, when the door from the bar banged open.

The drug addict appeared, framed by the weak light from the bar. Walker noted, with some admiration, that the girl had managed to un-holster his gun and had it trained on the man in the doorway, who shrank back.

"I heard noises, woke me up." He looked around the room, his mouth gaping. "What... what have you done?"

Walker went to speak, but the girl beat him to it.

"We haven't got time for this, Len! Have you got the gun?"

Len didn't answer; he simply stood there, gaping. Walker sighed and snatched his gun and holster from the girl and began moving the kegs to examine the bodies underneath. The veteran was dead, no doubt about that. A barrel had landed squarely on his head; all that remained was a crushed mess of red and black and a single, milky eye staring upwards, accusingly.

He stripped the greasy corpse of any valuables; nothing much, some coins, an old knife from the back pocket and a rusted hipflask. Walker sniffed its contents, got a foul whiff of turpentine, and threw it away. He turned to the body of the woman, there were no obvious wounds aside from a gash to her temple; she was breathing.

Walker clucked disapprovingly and pulled the knife back out. As he bent down to finish the body on the floor, the girl suddenly pushed him aside.

"Don't!" she cried. Walker could see tears running from under her visor, dark as blood in the dull light. "We've done enough, we should just leave." She checked the crumpled body at their feet.

Walker shook his head, "She knows us; we have to finish her or she will follow."

"They'll follow us *if* we kill her!"

The girl looked up at him; he saw himself mirrored in her visor, gun drawn, his own blood trickling from under his visor. He grunted and pocketed the knife again.

"Fine," He growled. "But we leave. Now." He stepped over the pool of blood soaking into the dusty concrete, stalked past the girl and pushed beanpole out of the way.

He heard the girl ask her brother about their gun again, as Walker surveyed the bar. It was blessedly empty; the patrons must have known that the couple were 'busy' out back; this probably meant that most of them were in on it. This meant they had to leave. A posse would come after them.

The other two had come in to the bar; she had retrieved her pistol and pouch from the bar, whilst he stood gaping stupidly.

"We have to go out the front, like nothing happened," Walker said, pulling his cloak around him to better disguise him. "If anyone else knew these people were robbing folk, then they'll be back to find out what loot they got."

The girl sniffed agreement, "People will be back to check, probably in about..." She trailed off, and eyed her feet as Walker gazed at her and he chuckled. He had thought there was more to her than all that noble 'real Philosophers' talk. He continued to look at her, until she scowled up at him from under her visor, "I did what I had to. To look after us"

Walker laughed again, shortly, and pulled some tobacco from his pouch, "And then you killed them. Cold."

He lit his cigarette and pointed to her brother, "Tell him to stop gawping like a moron and move."

Len looked around at Walker, and then ashamedly at the ground, "I never—"

His sister interrupted him, "That's enough, let's just leave already!"

She stormed past Walker and through the front door, her brother trailing after her. Walker went to follow, but paused and looked back towards the bar.

He leapt nimbly over the low counter and, after a moments rummage, found his books that the locals had swindled out of him earlier. He sanctimoniously blew the dirt from their covers, and replaced them one by one back into his satchel. He double checked the leather straps and the lock, habit guiding his hands through the ritual, and went to clamber back over the bar.

Out of the corner of his eye, he saw the bottle the old hag had poured from; the good one. No reason to leave good booze to these rubes, he reasoned. He reached up and claimed it and, after taking a deep swig, slung it into his hip pouch. He clambered back over the bar, following the siblings out into the night.

The morning sun was rising ahead of them, already blazing hot, as the three travellers made their way up the dusty slope. They had to move fast, which meant he had no time to cover their tracks properly. Unless they could get to the grey stone tower at the top of the hill they would be caught in the open by anyone following from the bar.

Walker paused and he scanned the horizon behind him. He could make out the main road through the town, where they had left earlier. There was activity there. He grunted and pressed a switch on the side of his visor; the lens zoomed in and he could make out the gang, gathering together in the shade of a building. Most of the men seemed to be local; thankfully none of the militia had been called. They were armed with pistols; one had a rifle, but what worried Walker were the two dogs. He hated dogs. He swore and flicked the stub of his cigarette away and began to lope up the hill, his boots hissing at the incline.

"Keep up," he ordered, moving quickly past the girl.

She was supporting her brother, who was suffering in the morning heat; clearly still feeling the effects of whatever drugs he was on, even now. Walker shook his head. The girl called after him, "You have to wait for us, Lenny can't move that fast!"

Walker ignored her and moved on; the tower was a good two hundred meters or so ahead; he needed to get there to set up. Hopefully they could hide, but he doubted it; a blind man could follow that clumsy oaf and his sister. He heard a groan and a dry thud and turned to look back at the girl, struggling to lift her brother from the dust.

"Get up, Len, we have to keep up with him!"

Her brother simply lay there, gasping and sweating in the baking heat. Walker looked back down the slope, towards the town. He could see a dust cloud, growing larger; the posse was moving out.

He scratched his chin and briefly considered his options. His two 'companions' below were definitely more of a hindrance than a help; the man was a wastrel; a drug addled fool, but the girl seemed handy in a fight, although she could end up being a lot of effort; too smart for her own good.

He cursed; he would need her gun, if it even worked, when fighting off the vengeful gang approaching from the town. Even if he left them, the gang would make short work of the two of them, and soon be after him.

Muttering to himself, he slid downwards and met with the girl. Without a word, he hoisted Len ungracefully onto his back, his armour hissing and squeaking in complaint, and began to work his way back up the slope. The girl simply stood and stared, eyes still hidden behind her visor, mouth slightly open.

Walker turned abruptly and growled, "Come on, for your mother's sake, I'm not doing this for my health." He began striding up the hill; the man weighed more than Walker would have guessed. Sweating, he called to the girl, who was catching up to his left, "You got that gun you pulled on me earlier, lass?"

He shifted Len's weight as he heard a click, the sound of a chamber housing being pulled back; she was checking it was loaded, "Yeah, I have a few rounds in the gun and some more in my pouch here."

Walker grunted his approval and continued up the hill. The tower was tantalisingly close now, and he dug in deeper and managed to clear the last hundred meters quickly, the girl easily following at his side. They crested the hill and moved quickly in to the relative shade of the tower's interior. Walker dumped Len on the gravelled ground and took stock of their surroundings, breathing heavily.

The tower had once been at least two storeys, but the top had been blown off; probably in one of the region's many wind storms. It was an old church, found almost everywhere before the Exodus. It was made of stones of irregular size, with solid, ancient wooden beams locked into the mostly collapsed ceiling. The stairs leading up to the higher levels were destroyed, but the ground floor had most of its walls intact.

The west facing wall was solid enough; there were large arched windows, perfect vantage points to fire from when the gang arrived. He checked the back wall, found it to be in worse condition.

Not entirely a bad thing; this could work to their advantage; openings in walls make for easy escape routes. He could easily leave at a moment's notice if necessary, or turn the crumbling mortar into a handy trap, and a tomb.

He turned to where the girl knelt, whispering to her brother. Walker heard him mention 'Flash' and he turned away disgustedly as she fed the weakling his fix, like an infant. He peered out of a westerly facing window. The mob was getting close; he could hear the mad barking of the hounds they were bringing after him. He loosed his pistol, and motioned to the girl.

"Make him quiet and get your gun over here, now. And remember, keep the sun to your back; stay in the shade of the tower."

She turned to him and nodded and, crouching low, made her way to the window next to Walker's; knelt and ready with her battered pistol drawn.

As the dogs leapt and strained against their leashes and the handlers sweated and swore in the heat, the girl could feel the hairs on the back of her neck stand up. She'd already had to kill one man, she wasn't sure she could do it again.

She swallowed and pushed her unease aside, flicking her hair from her face.

The walker knelt across from her, looking carefully out of the window to her left. He seemed calm, but no grin was on his lips. He stroked his chin thoughtfully and motioned to her. He held up four fingers, then two, and then three. She assumed this meant there were nine of them but they had not discussed hand signals before, so she had no idea.

He suddenly cocked his head, like a dog noticing something. She heard him curse, ever so softly, and he scratched his chin again. The girl hazarded a look herself. What she saw brought fresh waves of guilt and nausea.

Staggering up the hill, towards the back of the posse, was Bernie. Her head had swollen grossly from their fight in the keg-store; where she had been struck the flesh was purple and yellow, the wound was leaking; she could barely walk straight. Every now and then the madder of the two dogs would turn and bark at her, but she swatted at them with a length of scabby leather. The men around her looked both worried and angered; she would yell and scream obscenities at them, urging them forward.

The girl heard a quiet click as the walker carefully readied his pistol. She tried to follow suit, but her hand cannon was home made, and old. She tried to gently release the safety, but it clunked and whirred as the targeting lasers fired up automatically. It was too loud; the men beyond the wall heard. Shouting and firing randomly, the posse rained chaos on the girl and the walker.

Walker cursed again, louder, and shouted something at her, but she could not hear. He deftly slipped from his spot and fired through the window, knocking a heavy set, bearded man down to the ground, screaming and clutching his chest. The attackers responded, and the girl's ears seemed to shatter. Chunks of stone rained down, cutting her cheek and stinging her hand, which was shaking again. She had to stop them shaking; would Walker let her follow him if she couldn't even look after herself in a gunfight? She tried to visualise herself stepping out from cover and firing upon her attackers as Walker had, but could not. All she could picture was the veteran, crushed and dead in the bar, and Bernie, head swollen, body stumbling up the hill, like a monster from a nightmare.

She inhaled, deeply, and managed to peer out from cover. Bernie was still coming, screeching incoherently and flailing with her whip, the wound on her head shining sickeningly in the morning light. The girl exhaled, steeling herself, and swung from her position at the window to fire at a man leading a dog. She missed the handler, but the dog, a great, savage dark beast, howled woefully and died. She ducked back into cover as the owner retaliated; she could feel his rounds thudding into the wall behind her through her back, shaking her body, worsening her feeling of nausea.

Suddenly, she heard Walker again, louder, "I told you!" He bellowed.

The girl ducked as a salvo of shot flew through the window next to her; it pinged off into the tower, causing no damage but scaring her to hell. "What?" She screamed.

"I damn well told you," he repeated. "She followed us!"

He spat as a chunk of window frame splintered into dust, spattering his face. He stood and fired, anger etched in the hard lines of his mouth. The girl watched as Bernie's overripe head burst; her screams died into gurgles and she toppled to the ground, twitching.

She turned away from Walker back to her own window and found herself facing the other dog. All muscle and mad, animal rage, it launched itself ferociously through the window at her, knocking her to the ground and sending her gun flying, out of reach.

She screamed wordlessly.

The dog was on her chest, snapping viciously at her face; its weight pressed down on her, stopping her from breathing. The dog gnashed angrily, its teeth scraping off her visor, inches from her eyes.

Struggling to keep the weight of the dog's jaws from her face and throat, she screamed again, hoarsely, "Walker!"

She tried to look for the walker out of the corner of her eye, but he seemed to have gone. She swore inwardly and closed her eyes against the snarling maw, tried to close her nose from the reek of death. It rolled its mad eyes as its teeth smashed against her visor, drool pooling on its surface.

There was a crashing boom that filled her world, louder even than the dog's barking. She paused. The dog had stopped straining at her; it's dead weight was now on top of her and she couldn't move it.

She opened her eyes hesitantly, the sound of gunfire still ringing in her ears, and looked over to her right. Her brother stood there, her still smoking pistol held in his shaking hands. His eyes were wide, like a child with a new toy. The girl stared, open mouthed, "Thanks," she managed to gasp.

Daisy tried to sit, struggling to breathe, but her brother did not move to help her, "Hey, help me get this thing off of..."

But he had gone, leaping over her and the lifeless dog that was pinning her, and was outside before she knew what was going on. She cried out as best she could under the dog's weight and pushed, but couldn't shift it.

She heard excited laughter and the heavy gunshots of her homemade handgun; her brother had gone out there alone! He was going to get killed! She heaved once more, her desperation lending her a maddened strength, and finally managed to move the carcass.

She wriggled fiercely, finally struggling free. She leapt up and peered cautiously through the window. It looked clear enough, so she vaulted the ledge, landing lightly in a half crouch on the ground below. Her brother was dancing about like a madman, laughing and firing wildly upon the attackers, most of whom had either been shot or had run.

Staying low, she sidled as quickly as she could to one of the fallen enemies, the heavy man with the beard that Walker had first killed. She pulled his pistol from his grip and looked around for targets. She saw a couple of heads peeking over the brow of the hill, one in a duster and farmer's sun hat waving a pair of pistols, the other hairy, like a wild man, wielding a long, thin rifle. They were too far away for her but that rifle would be deadly for her and her brother. She yelled as he danced about like a lunatic.

"You'll have to get through me, first!" he bellowed at no one, shaking his fist and firing randomly.

"Lenny, get over here! It's not safe, it's—"

There was a crack of rifle fire, and her brother stopped dancing. The gun fell from his grasp, and he held his gut, slumping to his knees. He fell sideways sending a soft cloud of dust into the hot, still air.

Her stomach dropped.

She screamed a wordless curse and ran towards her brother, firing at the thing with the rifle. She could see the man desperately trying to reload. There was a loud crack and the man was snapped back, red blood glittering in the sun as it rained from the hole in his forehead.

As she ran across the open ground, away from the shadow of the tower and into the sun, the farm hat stood and made to fire upon her, but dropped suddenly, with two loud cracks. She ignored them and continued towards her brother, curled up against the dust and the pain. She slid next to him and held his head.

"Why did you do that?" She sobbed, stroking his hair.

She could still hear shouting, interspersed with gun shots, but she was focused on Lenny. She sat; stroking his hair, telling him it would be alright, trying to wipe the blood from his chin. She saw the red stickiness of his grubby, sweat stained shirt and looked into his rolling eyes; he was barely here, after all this, the flash still had him. A shadow fell over them, but she didn't turn.

"I told you to stay in the shade."

She didn't look up at him, but murmured softly to her brother instead, "Why, Lenny? Why did you do that?" She retracted her visor and looked down into her brother's dark brown eyes. She could see the handsome, strong boy he had once been. He coughed and smiled; he was still high, she thought wildly, feeling hope attempt to surface in her guts as she wondered if the flash might help.

He spoke, "D'you remember that time, we followed that man? Pointed a gun at my head... think he killed me..." He coughed, and blood spattered her leather half coat.

Still, she couldn't cry; even as her brother lay dying, she couldn't do it.

The walker spoke from behind her again, "You should kill him. Put him out of his misery."

She heard the flare of a match, and turned to him, disbelieving. "It's my brother," she choked.

The walker exhaled and rubbed his chin. "All well and good lass, but I reckon that's a gut shot. Fatal. Man'll be dead eventually, even if he's full of flash. But it'll be slow and painful, best you do him now and—"

She jumped up and stormed over to him. She drew her arm back and, with all she could muster, swung it upwards towards his chin. He caught it deftly and slammed her in the gut, hard, knocking the wind out of her. She collapsed, struggling to breathe, the tears gathered in the corner of her eyes, threatening to betray her.

He stood over her and adjusted his hat, "Don't try that again, girl. I like my face the way it is, and I didn't kill those men over there so you could live, and ruin it," He stepped over her, as she wriggled in the dirt, and drew his gun.

The girl tried her hardest to stand, but couldn't, collapsing awkwardly in the dirt.

"Now," The walker began, "you got two minutes to say your goodbyes, and all that. We need to leave now; some of those lads ran off and will be back, with more men. So you got one minute to catch your breath and another to say goodbye. Then you do it," he nodded to her brother, "Or I do."

The girl retched as she struggled to breathe, but managed to stand. She glared up at Walker, who stared impassively back, before limping back to her brother. She knelt and took his head in her lap again.

"How did we get here?" He asked her, eyes staring up into the sky, unseeing. "I thought mum and dad lost the home years ago?" He laughed, clearly remembering something from the hazy past.

The girl just sat, dumbly, as her brother slipped into delirium. At least he didn't seem to be in pain. Soon, he had stopped talking, and seemed to be sleeping fitfully, his breathing ragged.

The walker stepped forward, "Time's up, missy. He's just sufferin' now. You gonna take the shot or..."

She didn't answer, rubbing a grimy hand under her visor and grabbing her gun from the dust. She pointed it down at her brother, said a hoarse goodbye, and closed her eyes. There was another boom like a cannon, and Lenny was gone.

The girl shuddered, running her hand through her hair, blood from the day's work mingling with her sweat. So many dead, already, within a day of being with this man. And now what? Her home was gone; she had no friends, and now no family left. She had no choice but to follow Walker and hope he would take her to the Order, and didn't rob her, or kill her, or something equally horrible along the way.

She holstered her pistol, and turned to speak to the walker. He had already moved away, following the rising sun.

20 years ago...

The boy brandished his stick, waving it with worrying accuracy. Walker watched impassively as the creature warbled and yelped about water, defending what was his, and so on, before reaching forward and neatly plucking the stick from the boy's grasp.

The lad's face fell as Walker snapped it easily, and threw it aside. "Hey! That were my stick!". He sat heavily and began to sob. "It were mine, and it were the best one all 'round 'ere"

Walker sighed inwardly. "Look," he said, trying to keep his tone soft, "*You* threatened *me*, remember?"

The boy stopped sobbing and glared up at him, "You started it, coming down 'ere and trying to get me puddle off'f me. It's mine!"

He suddenly leapt to his feet and rushed at Walker, who simply grabbed the back of his scruffy shirt and lifted him, keeping him at arm's length.

The boy swung his arms fruitlessly, "'Ere, lemme go!"

Walker sighed again and rapped the boy lightly on the head with a knuckle, promptly causing him to stop swinging his arms. Walker waited a second, noting the thinness of the boy's face, the dirty brown hair and tattered ragged clothing. His bright blue eyes regarded Walker intelligently.

"Listen up, lad. How old are you?"

The grubby boy hung in Walker's grasp, thinking. "I'm... ten. I think. No one tells me. I just count when the leaves come down from the trees."

Walker looked down at the orphan, skinny in his threadbare vest, "I need a guide around town. Someone to show me the bars, shops, that sort of thing."

The boy looked slyly up at him. "Put me down an' I'll fink about it."

Walker obliged and, to his surprise, the little boy didn't run. Instead he placed a hand under his chin theatrically, obviously endeavouring to show deep thoughtfulness.

Walker had no time for games. "Well, boy? What's your answer?"

The boy grinned up at him, eyes glinting in the sun. "Do it for a penny, mister."

Walker rolled his eyes behind his visor, but dug into a pocket lining the inside of his cloak. He produced a battered, ancient copper piece. He held it out to the boy, but swiftly withdrew it, just in time. The boy was fast.

He hunkered down, visor level with the boy's sullen eyes, "You run, boy, and I'll catch you. Understand? I don't like being robbed."

The boy nodded and Walker flicked the coin into the air. He snatched it deftly from the air, and Walker nodded. The boy was fast indeed.

"Come on then, boy, let's go."

The boy scowled at the penny, trying to see if it was a fraud. After deciding all was good and proper, he nodded, pointing. "First pub's up 'ere. Smells a bit funny but they got nice old ciders."

The two walked up the dusty road, joining the other people wandering through the small town.

The boy piped up. "Wha's yer name then, mister?"

Walker glanced down at him. "Do names matter? I haven't asked yours."

The boy shrugged his skinny shoulders, and they carried on up the dusty road, towards the pub.

13

Walker had decided to let the girl tag along for a while, at least until the next city, or when he remembered why he had given her the book; whichever came first. Besides, she had proven useful once, and may do so again.

It had been two days since the skirmish at the tower and, fortunately, they had not been pursued further. The girl was still grieving over her brother, and Walker had left her to it. She seemed to be functioning still, doing tasks he asked of her and so on, but she wasn't talking.

The sun was rising on the third day, warming him up and promising to be long and dry, as usual. Walker, always the first to rise, rolled from the small shelter he had made with his cloak and stretched. His armour creaked and popped; he would need to find parts so he could repair it. He looked over to where the girl lay huddled among the roots of a gnarled oak tree, long dead but still standing.

Since the fight on the hill she would rarely raise her visor, hiding her misery behind the white-silver glare.

Walker checked the girl was definitely asleep before retracting his own visor. He prodded gingerly at his swollen cheek where the robbing old bastard had kicked him. He took his hat off and scratched his head. The hair there felt long and dirty. He sighed and replaced his hat and, reaching into the pack at his hip, retrieved his tobacco kit.

As he inhaled, the girl stirred and turned towards him, he hurriedly dropped his visor back, covering his eyes again, "Get up, lass. Time we were moving. If you need to do your business, go behind the tree, and hurry up."

She sat, looking at her knees. Walker sighed again. There was no time for grief. People died, especially out here, doing what he does. She had to learn. He turned from her and gathered his cloak, unfastening it from the gnarled tree he had slept against.

As he fastened it under the clasp on his chest, she spoke, "I'm hungry."

A smirk played on Walker's lips. He turned and grinned down at her, radiating good will, "Well, girl, all you had to do was ask."

He started to walk off, again following the sun eastwards.

She scrambled to her feet and called after him, "Hey! Aren't we eating? Please?"

He carried on, turning slightly, "No food here, lass. Next town shouldn't be far ahead. Keep up" He allowed himself another grin; hunger always drew people out; he knew she'd have to speak up eventually. He turned back towards the rising sun and slyly popped some hard bread into his mouth, chewing thoughtfully, wondering what town they would come to next, and how far it might be.

Trotting along nicely, he thought as his horse picked its way steadily along the old West road. It was still early in the day, but he could be at Windcombe in no time. Old Jenner down at the cider press would pay him extra, and maybe throw in some good, proper scrumpy too. His cart bumped and rattled, but his wife had insisted on packing the seats with rags and old clothes, turning the old hardwood bench into a fairly comfortable cushion.

He glanced over at his wife, Mary, who was reading one of her old books, silvery hair tied into a soft bun atop her head. She was rocking slightly with the sway of the cart, but seemed to be alright, considering she never usually made the trip out.

He smiled and looked over to the trees to his left, which marked the beginning of the fringe forest, separating the town from the main highway to the city, way behind him. They say robbers and bandits hid in there, awaiting people who looked like they had anything of value. But old 'Apples' Ollie had nothing of value, and therefore, Logic dictated (or so his wife told him), he had nothing to worry about. He'd never heard of this Logic chap, but he sounded nice enough, if a little dry, and so this didn't worry Ollie either.

He began to whistle, an old piece his wife had played back when she was still at work in the big city. As his cart rumbled merrily along, the sun rising behind him, he nibbled the food that Mary had packed for them. Fruit and bread mainly, but there was a bit of the ham left that they had had for dinner the other day. The thought of ole Jenner's scrumpy, along with the ham and the crusty bread made him happy, and he began to whistle anew, even as the trees thickened, making the road ahead darker. Heather continued to trot along, slightly slower now.

The formerly merry sound of his cart bumping and shaking started to take on a more ominous tone; his merry whistling was sucked into the yawning shadows amongst the trees. He trailed off, leaving a single, last note hanging in the air. Normally the woods were quiet, as woods generally are, but today seemed different, as if something among the trees was trying especially hard to be quiet. Ollie tried to whistle another few notes and pulled his cudgel closer. It was only a twisted piece of oak, but was hard as hell and better than a kick in the teeth. For Ollie at least.

Mary glanced up, noticing the cudgel, "What is it dear?" she asked.

Ollie tried to grin, "It's nothin' dear. Just being safe. Pop the book away a minute though, dunno who could be watchi—"

There was a sudden crack, causing him to yelp; Ollie grabbed the cudgel and looked about, breathing hard.

Mary clucked reproachfully, "Oh, stop worrying, you old goat. It's probably nothing, just an animal," she chuckled easily, turning back to her book, "No one would bother robbing us, everyone around here knows you."

She was right, of course. Bandits never bothered him; he knew a lot of them from the village, in fact, but quietly, of course (or on the down-low, as they liked to say). Still, say it was some other lads, not from his neighbourhood? Or someone worse?

There was another crack, snapping Ollie's thoughts back; his grip on the club tightened as something approached... he breathed a sigh of relief; it was a deer, looking more startled than he was.

He chuckled to himself and replaced the cudgel to the bench next to him. As he retook the reins, about to urge his horse on, he heard Mary gasp; there was a clunk and an evil metallic whir. He gulped.

"Easy now, old man" a soft voice said to his left.

He started moving his hand, slowly, toward his weapon, but was interrupted by a gravelly chuckle off to his right.

"I wouldn't do that if I were you fella," the gravel voice laughed, "She's fairly hungry, and liable to do strange things, being a woman and all."

He heard Mary whispering, but couldn't hear her over his own heartbeat. He didn't recognise the voices; so much for not being robbed.

He looked over at the first voice to his left and saw a young girl, dirty with travel and no older than twenty, skinny in her rough jeans and jerkin under a leather coat, short around her waist, holding a battered monster of a pistol.

She looked tired, from what he could see of her face; her eyes were covered by a slightly blinding shield of silver, and although her shoulders slumped, the pistol never wavered.

Ollie swallowed, terrified, but managed to speak, trying to sound brave, "What is it you want, then? Ole Apples got nothing o' value on his cart! You leave me an' the wife be, alright?"

The girl tilted her head to one side and motioned away to Ollie's right, amongst the trees, "You'll want to talk to him. He's the *boss*".

Even through his fear Ollie could sense the sarcasm. He stammered, "I... I..."

The gravel voice laughed again, and a man stepped from the gloom of the woods, causing Ollie's horse to shy and snort anxiously. He glanced at his wife, whose hands were also in the air, one still holding her book. It's funny, he thought, the details you remember when someone is pointing a gun at you. She was re-reading her old musicology books; the page had flopped open onto a bloke called Beethoven, which sounded like a vegetable to Ollie. He was sure he could remember Mary playing it to him, back in the day. Oh how he used to love her playing...

He was brought out of his badly timed introspection by the man's voice. Ollie's eyes flicked back to him, taking him in. He was rough looking, tall too, wearing a weather stained leather cloak about his neck, where it was fastened beneath a clasp on some battered military armour, which was scratched and rusted along the plates that led down his chest. Ollie could make out a dark shoulder bag, bulging with heavy, square shapes. The man was wearing a visor too, like the girls, but darker, and an old, wide brimmed hat on his head. Ollie's eyes widened, "You... You're one of them? A walker?"

He glanced nervously back at the girl, who was still holding her gun up, pointed at his head. He turned back to the walker, whose face had widened into a smirk.

Ollie continued, desperately, "I ain't got no books, or nothin'! Just fruit, honest!"

The Walker continued to beam at him and beckoned them down, "Come on now, Sir, Ma'am." He took his hat off when he spoke to Mary, showing short dark hair, curly and dirty looking. The visor over his eyes went back along his head, disappearing into the matted hair.

"We're not gonna hurt you. The girly is new to this, hence the gun. Why don't you come down off that cart, we just want to talk."

"Wait, I got ham too! You two can just take it, leave us be? The book the Wife's got? Nuffin, just music and that!"

Ollie looked pleadingly at the man, who continued to smile disarmingly, beckoning him down a second time with another wave.

"Come on, Ollie," his wife spoke, smiling at him, "Looks like we haven't got much choice."

She placed her book beside her on the cushioned bench and started to climb down. The rough man stepped forward.

Ollie yelled, brandishing his club. The horse started, snorting loudly. "Don't you hurt her mister! Or I'll whack you on the head so hard yer teeth'll fall out!"

There was a loud whine, unnoticed by Ollie, and the walker looked up at him, slowly. He then offered his hand up to Mary, "Only offering the lady a hand mister; a fall from that height, she could twist an ankle, or worse."

Mary looked at Ollie, and smiled again, "I'll be alright dear. But put the stick down; the young lady doesn't seem too impressed."

Ollie looked back at the girl and, slowly, ever so carefully, put the club back down on the bench. She was still pointing the gun at him, but this time a red light was coming from under the barrel. The gun was whirring and clicking; it sounded like it was under quite a lot of pressure.

Ollie grinned nervously and climbed off the cushioned bench and onto the leafy ground. The man with the gravelly voice finished helping Mary down, and the two of them made their way around the front of the cart, past Heather.

She snapped at him, causing the man to flinch, momentarily losing his cool smile. The walker scowled at it, mumbled something under his breath and brushed his cloak. He resumed his course, albeit further away from the horse, giving the animal a wide berth. He reached Ollie's side and nodded towards her.

"Horrible, stupid creatures." he said amicably, looking down towards the cigarette he was rolling.

Ollie thought about this, and began his reply, "Well, mister, Heather's actually pretty clever, especially when it comes to readin' people. F'r instance, she'll snap at anyone who's a bit of a bastar— Ouch!"

Mary leaned forward, smiling brightly, as Ollie swore quietly and clutched at his foot.

"Mr Walker, what I'm sure my husband meant was that Heather's had a long old morning, and could've snapped at anyone." She turned sternly back to Ollie. "Isn't that right, *dear*?"

The man looked evenly up at them, nodding, "That's right, Mister Apples, you've been doing well so far. Don't upset me now."

The walker lit his cigarette and inhaled deeply. He suddenly resumed his smile and clapped Ollie on the shoulder in a gesture of open friendliness that Ollie was entirely sure wasn't genuine.

Ollie nodded and made a zipping motion across his mouth and nodded vigorously.

The walker turned nonchalantly to the girl, who was still pointing her straining gun at Ollie. "Turn the overcharge off. The whine is annoying me."

After a few moments the girl complied, flicking a switch on the side of her gun, which she lowered slightly. A cloud of something puffed from the gun, and the keening note died down, returning the previous quiet to the woods.

"Now, we don't want trouble. Just a trade." The man opened the satchel hanging from his shoulder, undoing the metal clasps and pulling the leather thongs loose. It was full of books, papers, scrolls; more than Ollie thought anyone would need. He had no idea what these people could want.

He interrupted, wringing his hands nervously, "I tole you mister, the book Mary had ain't worth a thing. All we gots are me apples and me lunch. You're welcome to both, so long as you don't hurt us."

The man ignored him, turning to his wife, "You like music, Ma'am?"

Mary glanced at the book on the seat behind her and nodded. "Yes," she said, eyeing him quizzically, "I was a musical technician for a governor once, down South. A long time ago now."

The walker began to whistle slightly, the same song Ollie himself had earlier. He rummaged briefly in the sack and produced some loose pages, along with a slim volume. He offered them to Mary, who took them, staring. The walker stopped whistling and waited.

Ollie strained on his tip toes to see what was on the pages his wife was studying; they had groups of long straight lines going across the page, with little dots, dashes and other strange symbols. Below the bars were words. Although he couldn't read it upside down, he recognised it.

"This is sheet music!" Mary cried happily, troubles momentarily forgotten, "Sonata no.14, in C-sharp! The nocturnes! Oh, the minor ones though. Oh, and look Ollie, a book on old world instruments," She smiled up at the walker, "How thoughtful."

He smiled back and turned back to Ollie, who looked up at him, eyebrow arched. "First you threatens us, then you gives us this... stuff. What do you want, mister?"

Mary had clambered back up to her seat on the cart, quite forgetting the current dangers. She called down at him, "Give him as many apples as he needs, Oliver," he flinched at the use of his full name, "These pages are worth more than your apples."

Although Ollie severely doubted that pages, pages which he couldn't read, could be worth more than a tonne of apples, he loved his wife dearly and decided not to argue. He also loved his life dearly, and decided that if she wanted whatever the heavily armed strangers in front of him wanted, then it was all well and good, and a happy coincidence too. He climbed back up to his seat, completely forgetting about the man, or the girl with her ramshackle gun.

He sighed, "Yes, dear. So what's it you wanted then, fella? Like I said, only got apples and ham."

The man opened his mouth to reply, but the girl cut in, "I'd quite like some food."

Ollie looked down. She did look unwell, "How long's it been since you ate, girl?"

He saw her mouth turn down in displeasure. "Don't call me that. That's what he calls me," she nodded towards the big man next to her, who shrugged. "My name's not *girl*, it's Daisy. Sorry about the gun. Like Walker said, I'm *new* to this."

Ollie smiled weakly, ignoring the venomous sarcasm, hoping it wasn't aimed at him, and looked back to man, "So, you *are* a walker. With the Order?"

He saw Walker's smile flicker briefly. When it returned it was no longer friendly. It was reptilian.

"Now *Oliver*," he replied, emphasising the name, "You know it's illegal to distribute information to people like you, out here, unless you're a member. So what do you think?"He exhaled and flicked his cigarette away meaningfully.

Ollie thought about this and changed the subject, turning back to the girl, "Okey-dokey... Daisy, I have plenty of apples, as you can see," he motioned towards the open cart behind him.

Mary was still engrossed in the pages Walker had given her, but she nudged him with an elbow. "Oh yeah, and the ham, I suppose," he continued unenthusiastically.

Daisy stood up straighter, "I'll have the ham then, thanks," she said brightly. She grinned up at him from under her shining visor.

Walker smiled too, normally this time, and said, "And the bread you mentioned as well please, Ollie."

Ollie nodded, glumly. He had been looking forward to that. But at least he still had the scrumpy to look forward to, later on.

He fished around in his lunch sack and produced the crusty bread and the ham, which was wrapped in brown paper. He handed it down, where it was taken by the girl. Before she ate though, she offered the food to Walker. When he shook his head, she hungrily attacked the bread, pausing only to take bites of ham. Ollie watched, astonished.

"You were right, Walker. She was hungry. I've never seen a lady eat like that. Where are you two headed then?" he asked.

Walker had rolled another cigarette during the exchange. He lit it and puffed gently, looping his hands into his belt. He looked up at Ollie and turned his head east, "That way, towards the next town."

Ollie nodded, "Back that way's my village, little place. We owns the orchard there. Treach Orchard, 's'called. Had a book on it once, writ by my pa's pa," he glanced at Walker, "long time ago, 'course," he added hurriedly. "Very old buildings there abouts, very interestin'—"

Walker interrupted him with a wave, "I don't care for old buildings, Apples. We need to get to the city." He took another drag on his cigarette and turned back to Ollie, "Actually, that's what I wanted to talk to you about."

Ollie didn't like the sound of that, "What do you mean, Mister Walker?"

Walker leaned on the cart, next to Ollie, and exhaled smoke, "We need to borrow your cart. Long way to the city, right?"

Ollie looked down at him, waving the smoke from his face. The man was a maniac, of course. The city was... well, a bloody long way away and there was no way he'd take him for some poxy old pages, no matter what his wife said. He opened his mouth to object, but the Walker had opened his satchel again and produced a book.

"I know what you're going to say, Ollie, and I agree. It is a long, long way to the city. And I would never ask you to take us all the way for some sheet music, no matter how valuable they may be to the lady," he looked at Mary and nodded, who nodded back happily, before returning his gaze to Ollie. "What was your full name Ollie?"

Ollie paused, confused. "Olliver Treach. We would get confused at tea times, me and me pa, on account of us having the same name, sort of thing."

Walker nodded and continued rummaging. "Well, you'll be relieved to hear that I only want to go as far as the border of the local township; your village. And you can have this."

He offered the familiar book up to Ollie, who took it gingerly. It had no writing on its cover and was heavy, bound in old, cracked book leather. Mary leaned over him and peered at it.

"What is it, dear?" she asked.

Walker answered, as Ollie opened and leafed through the pages. "It's recipes for apples. Cider, cider wine, vinegars, cakes, pies. Pretty much anything that can be done with an apple. Oh, there's a nice cider whiskey in there, if you think you can make it. It's yours. You should show it to whatever brewer or pub you were taking these too. Was originally written around here as well, if I'm not mistaken."

He thumped the apple cart before vaulting in, leaving Ollie with the book. He couldn't believe it, the chances this stranger, this walker having this book, *this* book, of all books...he hadn't seen it for over forty years and... well... he noticed Mary was staring at him. He wiped his eyes and smiled at her.

"What's the matter, dear?" she placed a hand on his arm, "What are you going to do?"

He turned to look at his passenger, "Thank you Walker, you've done me a good service. You two are certainly strange, but we'll take you to the township all the same, as far as you need."

As the girl scrambled into the cart, clutching what was left of the bread and ham, the walker tipped his hat and settled down amongst the apples.

Ollie turned back and looked at the book, which he'd opened to the first page. It was still there. His grandfather's signature hadn't worn away at all. Ollie smiled again and placed the book into his lunch sack, took the reins, and gently steered Heather around, carrying the walker where he needed to go.

Daisy watched Walker from under her visor. She had started sleeping in it, just like her travelling companion, who never seemed to take his off at all; she wondered idly at this, trying to get comfortable amongst the apples.

He currently seemed to be sleeping, his wide brimmed hat pulled down over his face. He had traded some pages and a book, which had been enough to get them transport to the next town, for which she was quietly grateful; the man set a mean pace and she was exhausted. He would wake early, stop late and hardly seemed to eat. The food had been scarce, not that this had seemed to affect him at all.

She had finished the bread and ham, and now nibbled quietly at an apple while the carter and his wife argued about something uninteresting up front. It was hard and sour; a cider apple. She threw it from the cart and resumed her study of Walker. She could smell him still, over the pungent tang of the apples, but she had started to get used to it. It wasn't an entirely bad smell, just the smell of one living on the move all the time.

They hadn't managed to stop to bathe yet, although Walker seemed less fazed by this than she was. In all fairness she wasn't sure that she smelled exactly like a bed of roses, or a cartload of apples rather, when it came down to it.

Daisy sighed and looked out at the scenery. They had left the dried forest and returned to a vista of sparse, rugged grass, more yellow and brown than green, and were heading downhill towards a small town, which stood by a river. Ollie the cart driver had told her this was, or had once been, called the river Avon, which the man's wife had assured her meant river in some ancient language, which in turn meant that the river was called the river River, which seemed strange. Lenny would have... she stopped herself, and sighed again, sadly.

She missed her brother, but what hurt her more is her realisation that, if he hadn't died himself, she would have probably died instead; she wasn't sure whether she should be grateful or saddened by this. And Walker would have never taken the two of them. He didn't seem like a man who entertained fools gladly.

She unholstered her gun, the home made hand-cannon, and ran her hand over the scratched metal of the barrel. Her brother had made it, back when she had been far too small to hold it up. She remembered how he taught her to shoot, and laughed when she could barely aim it or keep it level.

Her hand passed down the fraying leather strap tied around the grip, and found the tag there. It was a smiling face, faded yellow with black eyes and broad, jolly smile. It too was scratched, more silver shone through than yellow now, but that didn't matter. She had no idea why he'd put it on there, but then, he'd been a simple guy. Maybe he'd just liked the smile.

Walker grunted, and she hurriedly put her gun away. He didn't stir for a while. She watched the man's wide jaw, muscles rippling as he grumbled to himself. He abruptly stopped and reached behind him, rummaging. Ollie called from the front, "Hey, Mister? Nearly at the town, so you might wanna pack up."

Walker ignored him, focused on finding whatever had woken him from his sleep. Daisy watched, interested.

Ollie turned back, to see if they had heard him. He noticed Walker's rummaging, and groaned, "Oh, bloody 'ell, tell me you ain't found one of them weevils. Bloody evil buggers gets bigger each year, I'm sure of it"

Walker stopped rummaging and, slowly and carefully, pulled out a knobbly apple, all angles where there should be none. He considered it for some time. Then he took a bite.

He told Ollie to pull the cart up, between mouthfuls of sour apple. The journey had taken two hours, which was easily six or so hours walking. As they clambered down from the cart, Walker turned to look at the little white haired man, still sat on his high bench behind the horse.

"You know any where I can hire water transport down there, Ollie?"

Daisy looked up at the man, as he stroked his bushy white beard, "Hmmm," he said, "There's a young man down there, goes by the name o' Tim, or Tom, or summing similar"

"Tom, you old fool," Mary cut in. She continued, "He took over from his grandfather when he died; Ollie and I knew him. It's a ship called *The Good Gel*, follows the Avon both ways. You should speak to him; it's probably down on the river. Bright red, if I remember correctly, you couldn't miss it."

"It's more of a boat, really," added Ollie.

Walker nodded and began to walk down the slope towards the town, crunching his apple loudly.

Ollie shook his head, "Not even a thank you." He muttered.

His wife pushed his arm, gently. "He paid us plenty Oliver, and you know it."

He shrugged his agreement, and the two of them turned to Daisy.

She had grown a little fond of the two of them; he was as common as the apples he carted, loved cider and was grumpy, she was well read, well spoken and had an almost regal look about her. She smiled sadly and thanked the two of them and turned to follow Walker.

Mary called after her, "Why are you following that man, young lady?"

Daisy looked at them from behind her visor. She wasn't going to tell them about her family, or her quest. As nice as these people seemed, the less people knew the better off she was.

"I've got nothing else." Was all she could think to say.

Mary looked at her; Daisy couldn't quite read her expression. "Just be wary. What you've heard about the Walkers may not be as true as you'd think. You're too young to remember..." she looked away slightly, but turned back abruptly. "Just take care."

Ollie clucked and snapped the reins slightly, starting his cart turning away. Daisy stood and watched as they moved away slowly up the road. She didn't watch them all the way; she knew that the walker wouldn't wait for her.

16

Walker strode down the hill, the early midday sun stretching his shadow behind him. The girl had caught up and was walking easily by his side. Some of her colour had come back and she had started talking again. He had learned her name too; Daisy. Not that it would matter.

He had decided to see what she knew about the Walkers, and the Order, and would ask questions that might help jog his memory as to why he had given her the book those ten years ago. Small talk first. "Your brother died a good death."

She didn't reply; for a while they walked in silence, the comment hung between them like the bloated corpse of a criminal.

He had thought she would react to some praise for the wastrel. The only sound was of the crickets underfoot, chirping angrily as their boot steps interrupted whatever it was crickets did.

Eventually, she replied. "He was just simple. He tried to help. "She looked quickly towards Walker.

"Thanks, I guess."

They walked along quietly for a few more minutes. Walker was enjoying stretching his legs after the cramped, sour smelling cart journey, as well as being away from that foul horse. Damn thing had nearly bitten him; could've taken his fingers off. He mulled his next question over in his head.

"You did well, back at the church. Where did you learn to shoot like that?"

She merely shrugged. Walker rubbed at his chin as they strode through the brush. "Not many people can shoot that well girl." He coughed when she didn't reply. "You should be pleased. Took me some time before I learned to use a weapon like that."

Again, she didn't respond, so Walker lapsed back into silence. He needed to know what she knew, but this idle chat was getting him nowhere; he decided on the direct approach. "So, girl, what did your pappy tell you? About the Order, and the Walkers?"

She turned to him as they ambled down the hill, her visor reflecting the rising sun ahead. "Not much," she replied, "only that you work to gather knowledge."

Walker scratched his chin, "So, do you know why some people say walkers, and others say the Order?"

Daisy carried on alongside him, thinking. "Well, I'm not sure. I always assumed there wasn't a difference. Just some of you call yourselves Walkers, and some of you say the Order. I assumed it was a rank thing. Although," she added, tilting her head slightly at him, "my dad did tell me some of you were good, and the rest of you were bad. He always said it was the bad ones that came to our village and..." She trailed off.

Walker smiled to himself; the girl still thought of things as 'good' or 'bad'. This could work well for him. She also seemed to think that the Walkers and the Order were one and the same. He plucked another apple from a pocket sewn into his cloak. They were sour, but he quite liked the sharpness.

He took a bite, chewed, and pulled the rest of the worm from his apple. Unperturbed, he continued, "So, you don't know a lot of our history then? You don't know about me?"

She shook her head. "Why would I know about you?"

He shrugged, so she continued. "Well, no. I only know about the Walkers from my Dad. So... No, I don't really know."

He nodded, satisfied. The less she knew, the better. "And what is it you're doing, then?" He looked down at her.

She certainly looked healthier for the rest in the cart. She had been hungrier than he had realised.

She patted the front of her jeans as she walked, thinking. "Well, you're the one that gave me the book. I thought you were taking me to the Order. Aren't you?"

Walker said nothing, continuing to chew, so she pressed on. "You can get me in, so I can start training. You're a walker. Hence the name, right?"

Walker swallowed and looked out towards the horizon. "I never said anyth..." he trailed off.

Something had caught his eye. He flung the apple core from him and stopped abruptly, the girl carried on a few steps. She paused ahead of him and turned.

"What is it?" she asked curiously.

There was a truck headed towards them from the town, dark smoke billowing from its exhaust. He flicked the switch on his visor and zoomed in, Daisy's questions going unanswered. The truck was all black, spattered with mud and dust from the road. It looked fairly modern; more modern than anything the locals could afford. The sun gleamed from the convex windshield covering the bubble cockpit as the four heavy wheels at the back churned up the ground, spraying dirt and debris behind it. He swore and dropped to a crouch.

"Bookmen. Coming up the road. Quickly, down." He pulled her down, ignoring her protests. He began to move to his right, along the hill and away from the road they had been walking down, dragging the girl along behind him.

"Why are we hiding? Can't you just talk to them? Hey!" she pulled free of his grip and went to stand.

"If you stand," he growled, "Those men will be the last of your worries." She looked down at him and flicked her visor up, worried eyes scanning what she could see of his face. She stayed crouched, obviously deciding that he wasn't playing around.

"Come on." He motioned and led the way, the rumble of the truck growing louder as it clambered up the hill.

Luck, as usual, was on his side; he had found a ditch, probably some remnant from old farmland, the area had probably been agricultural pre-strife. He pulled her down beside him and placed a finger on his lips. She nodded and hunkered down. Walker removed his hat and gingerly peered over the top of the ditch.

The truck was just reaching the spot they had been standing, and was coming to a stop. Walker could hear voices from the cab. The nearside door opened and a man, clad in modern power armour, dropped lightly to the ground. He stood straight, his full black suit gleaming darkly in the midday sun. Most of his face was hidden by a rounded full faced helmet, the visor a material similar to the girl's visor, silver and shining, compared to Walker's older dulled gun metal grey; his jaw sat proud of the visor, grim mouth assessing the landscape.

"I'm telling you," he was saying to his companion, who had remained in the truck, "I saw someone, I'm sure."

His companion sighed audibly. "It's not our job to harass people farting about in fields though, is it mate?"

The first man turned from his examination of the ground and pointed at his colleague. "Maybe, whoever it was, was wearing Order clothes," he tapped his helmet, "The hat and that."

He turned back to his colleague in the truck, "and I told you about that! When we're working, its Sergeant, got it?

"It's just us two, there's no need for that is there?" his companion wheedled.

The first man waggled his finger "It's called discipline, Corporal, discipline is what makes this organisation strong. Besides, what if someone heard us? What if that person I saw *was* of the Order? It'd be fraternising, or something."

The corporal leaned over from the driver's seat. Walker could see all of the man's ratty face, he wasn't wearing his helmet. "Come on, *sergeant*," he moaned sarcastically, "There's no one here, *sergeant*. We've got places to be, *sergeant*."

The sergeant had been moving closer to the ditch, but turned angrily and, to Walker's relief, began to climb aboard the vehicle. "Less of the sarcasm, you little wan —" His voice was cut off by the door slamming. The bass of the engine rumbled deeply and the truck trundled off up the road.

Walker exhaled. He thumbed tobacco from his pouch and started to roll himself a cigarette. Was that what the Order was working with these days? He'd been away from the capital too long.

"They've gone," he grunted.

Daisy stood slowly, looking towards the road. "Why did you hide from them?" she asked him.

He licked the paper on his cigarette, and put it between his lips. He lit it, shook out the match and climbed out of the ditch. As she scrambled up behind him, he turned and watched the truck disappear over the crest of the hill. He turned and started his way back down the hill, avoiding the road.

"Well?" she pressed, "you can't just ignore me, you know."

He didn't stop as he replied, "They might be what *you* would call the 'bad guys'".

20 years ago...

It had been three months since Walker had met the boy. He had turned out to be helpful, and Walker liked people who were helpful; he could use them. Besides, he had seen potential, a possible talent he could nurture. And the boy was keen; there was no doubt about it. He could do well, given the time.

Already he was quick, mentally and physically. Walker watched as the boy loped ahead, carrying the pack of supplies Walker insisted he carried, in order to build his strength. He whistled and the lad stopped, turning to him.

"Making good time today, Walker. Nearly at the next town." He beamed proudly.

The boy's speech had come on leaps and bounds too; he would start learning to write next. If he did well, Walker thought, he'll start his martial training. But he had to show him something first.

"Come on, boy, there's something we need to do."

The boy frowned, turning back to look at the town just on the horizon. "But... we're nearly there. We could be there by noon!"

Walker ignored him and made his way into the woods to the left of the track they had been following. He listened for the noises of the boy following and, sure enough, was met by the sounds of undergrowth being trampled and slapped about.

"Stop playing, boy. I told you, remember to keep quiet at all times. You never know when someone may be near, watching."

The boy didn't respond, but Walker was pleased to note that the noises died to almost nothing. He was learning quickly indeed.

Walker held up a hand and stopped at the edge of a clearing. In the centre was a dilapidated husk of a building, a remnant of the old world, forgotten and unloved. It was once huge, but most of its high walls had fallen, leaving only the front and the far side standing whole. Some of the wording that had once sat atop the building had been lost, leaving only "PUBLISHING" left. What had once assumedly been an adorable mascot-creature was now merely a rusted goblin, squatting grimly alongside the text, as worn by time as the building on which it stood.

Walker looked at it. "What do you see, boy?"

The boy joined him, head nearly at Walker's shoulder. He scratched his chin, habitual when he was thinking, and murmured. "Well, I know the first bit, pub, like wheres we gets whiskey,"

Walker interrupted, "You mean, 'like a pub, where we get whiskey'. You know what happens if you don't speak properly, lad."

The boy rolled his eyes, spat and continued. "Yes. The rest I don't know. What's that next to it?"

He pointed up to the bird. Walker studied it for a moment, then shrugged. "An emblem of the past, who knows? What is more important is what once happened at this place. Come on."

He motioned that the boy should follow, and headed towards the building, heading right and into the rubble. The boy scrambled after him as they climbed, first up the mound, and then in to the building. Bricks and concrete moved beneath the boy's feet, but Walker's stride was true as ever. The boy slipped as some of the rubble shifted beneath him. He caught his knee and swore.

"Think about where you put your feet, and you won't fall," He said without looking back, "And swear again and you'll taste leather."

The boy nodded, gritting his teeth and fighting back tears at the pain in his knee. He moved slower, deliberately, like Walker, and found his footing much more stable. The old man knew his stuff. "Hey Walker," he called.

Walker waved him quiet, and pointed into the gloom of the collapsed building. "See that, boy?"

The boy squinted into the darkness. He could make out something big; thin cylinders arranged at intervals all attached to a big metal box. There were long, continuous sheets draped from roller to roller. He got the feeling that this room had had some deeper power, long ago. It felt like it may still be here. He licked his lips.

"Whassat then?" he asked.

Walker turned slowly to him. "It *was*," he began quietly, "A source of knowledge."

The boy rubbed his chin. "What, a big metal dead thing?"

Walker shook his head. "Come on, closer."

He strode down into the shadows, leaving the boy standing nervously behind. Part of him wanted to stay behind, out of the dark and away from the huge thing. But a bigger part of him wanted to know what Walker meant. A source of knowledge. He licked his lips again and hurried down the rubble, into the shadows.

He found Walker by one of the rollers, which was lying discarded on the ground like a lost limb. The sheet was still tangled around it, and Walker was holding a part of it up.

45

"Touch it." He ordered.

The boy refused, holding his hands behind his back.

Walker laughed. "Go on, it's not a trick. I'm holding it."

The boy swallowed and touched it. He recognised the roughness. "Paper?" he ventured, looking up at Walker.

Walker smiled down at him and nodded. "Paper. It's lasted so long. Probably due to the weather." He paused, "Well, lack of it."

The boy felt the paper, thick and hard in his hands, "Why does it feel so different?"

Walker ignored him, looking around, "This place was a publishing house. It's where books were printed."

The boy stopped rubbing the paper and looked up at him. "Books? Them things with words in? I thought they was bad?"

Walker shook his head and headed back towards the sunlight outside, the boy following at his feet. They reached the top of the mound and stopped, looking back to the printing machine in its collapsed home.

"Once, books were everywhere," Walker said softly.

The boy watched with baited breath as Walker began to undo the clasps on his satchel. He had always wondered what the man had kept in there, what he felt was worth protecting so secretly. Walker dug into the pack and drew out a book. It wasn't a very big one, and its sad red sleeve was ruined and illegible, but it was still a book.

Walker looked down at the boy, and held the book out. He reached out for it, but Walker sharply drew it back.

"Tell me, boy, do you know of the Philosophers?"

The boy stared at the book, but answered, "Yeah, the other kids back home talked about them. They said their mums and dads told them about people what went around gatherin' books up and makin' them safe. Or summink"

The last grammatical slip earned him a wallop.

The boy rubbed the back of his head, scowling up at Walker, who said, "That's almost right. All you need to know is that that's what we do. Protect books. Share them around. Knowledge is power now, it's all we have left. If these go," Walker brandished the book at him, making him flinch, "We can never get them back. No sonatas, no Descartes, no King. When books die," he put the book back into his satchel, "History dies." And if history dies, we have nothing left. No way to move forward. To rebuild," he gestured about him, "All of this. You understand?"

The boy nodded slowly, now staring at Walkers satchel. "So, what you mean is, if we has books, we has knowledge, and history and all that stuff," Walker raised a grammar correcting hand, but the boy darted nimbly away, "And if we *have*," he emphasised the word, "all that stuff, then we can change things?"

Walker nodded and smiled, despite himself. "That's near enough right. Knowledge is power, boy. Remember it. It's probably the most important resource left to us. With the right knowledge, anything is possible."

Walker began to make his way down the mound of rubble, back towards the road, leaving the boy behind, watching him and rubbing his chin thoughtfully.

18

Tom stood on his boat, hands on his hips and angry. No cargo, no passengers and those two troopers had come and ransacked his home, while he'd been out. He bellowed for his cabin boy, George. Well, Tom thought, he wasn't really a *boy* anymore, *per se*, but saying cabin man just felt, well, wrong.

George stooped as he came from below deck, stopping halfway up the steps that lead up.

"Sorry Tom," he said, "I was cleaning out the mess those chickens made yesterday."

Tom screwed his eyes up. Those damned birds hadn't been worth the money they had brought him. Loud, smelly, messy and, and, the bloody cheek of it, the owner had demanded they stay in his personal quarters. Chickens! In the captains quarters! Not that he had any quarters to speak of, but still, unbelievable. He had been tempted by the owner's money, which had, upon closer inspection, turned out to be fake.

Although it had been Tom who had taken the money, he naturally blamed George, as any good captain would.

"George, hurry up and finish cleanin that bloody hold, I want to be able to eat off of the floor!" he'd heard words to that effect when he was in the army, but relating to toilet seats, which Tom considered too unsanitary for dining upon.

"What will you be eatin' Tom?" George asked. He stood there, all seven foot of him, eye to eye with Tom who was standing on the deck above him, by the tiller.

"Why do you ask? Just scrub that chicken sh— chicken business off of my floor, for goodness sake!"

George frowned, "Well, since we have no money, you won't be eating anything off of the floor or otherwise, unless you like eatin' chicken shit. So, my reasoning being," he reasoned, "there's no real rush to clean it off, since, were I to clean it all up, you'd be unable to eat it, seeing as it'd all been cleaned up, and would therefore have nothing to eat off of the floor. See?"

Tom's mouth worked through this, slowly turning each word over like a stone, mentally prepared to flinch from the insects that would invariably scuttle from underneath.

He wasn't sure if George was winding him up or not. Sure, he sloped about the place, chuckling at mundane things, fart noises and funny shaped vegetables, but every now and then he would come out with a piece of thinking so sound that it made Tom stop and think. He recovered quickly, however,

"Look, George, clean the crap off the floor and I'll buy you a pint later."

George smiled, clearly forgetting his recent foray into financial logic. "Cor, thanks Tommo! Hey, I just thought of something. Chicken crap, it's fowl-ness! Geddit?" He laughed heartily and made his way below decks, as Tom breathed, relieved. Order had been restored.

He looked about him. His ship, well... his boat, *The Good Gel*, was empty aside from himself, the steering wheel beside him, and George, below. The deck was narrow and long, perfect for carrying cargo that preferably didn't move or defecate all over the place. She had been painted red once, a long time ago, but the sun had bleached her to a none too unpleasant pink, which Tom rather liked.

He walked to the rear of the ship, which was the stern when Tom remembered to be a captain and not a civilian, and slumped onto the engine. That had been another waste of money. She was bloody ancient, and therefore bloody expensive; powered by petrol, the real stuff, which was almost impossible to come by. It was a shame that vege diesel hadn't worked either. If only he'd think things through more. He sighed and patted the metal beneath him.

The petrol situation meant that they relied solely on wind power, which wasn't too bad; the natural wind tunnel of the valley sped them along nicely, but the engine would have sped them a bit more speedily, and even more nicely.

He picked his nose despondently. He could hear George singing away happily to himself below, his booming valleys voice vibrating the deck. Maybe he'd have to sell the old girl, he thought gloomily. It would be a shame, since she's been in the family so long — His train of thought was interrupted by a sudden shout from the shore.

"You, on the boat. Looking for a fella named Tom, you know him?" The man shouting was tall and wrapped in a dark brown cloak, travel stained and beaten. He wore an old hat and faded blue jeans. He was walking down the gangway towards him, with a young lady, also in faded work jeans. Tom lifted his cap and squinted. They were both wearing similar looking face gear, which he recognised.

"Not for peoples like you, I'm afraid." He spat overboard, and continued, "Government types got their own travel. I'd hate to waste a journey, people here are desperate to get down the river."

The man looked about him slowly, spreading his arms.

The sun gleaming dully from his visor as he spoke, "Lucky us. Looks like we *just* missed the lunchtime rush, Tom. But I'd hate for two foolish latecomers with *paying* business to interrupt your banquet in the hold."

Tom opened his mouth to retort, but couldn't think of anything to say.

"Before you ask, Tom, I could hear you long before I could see you. This your boat?" The man shook his head and climbed the gangplank.

"Terrible."

Tom's jaw dropped like a man in a head high circular saw factory. Who did this bloke think he was? Steppin' on a man's boat uninvited, only to insult him? The bloody cheek!

"George?" he yelled, finally remembering how to speak and reaching for his fish knife in his back pocket, "Get up 'ere! We got guests!"

He pointed at the man, still fumbling with the knife stuck on his belt loop, and was about to tell him 'how much he was going to regret this' when the man snatched forward and grabbed his finger, forced it back. All Tom managed was a heartfelt groan, before he was forced down to his knees.

George appeared from below, smiling amiably.

"Hullo!" he grinned, seemingly oblivious to Tom's plight, "I do like guests. I'll pop the kettle on, shall I Tommo?" he disappeared again, whistling.

The man maintained his grip on Tom's fingers, whose eyes had started to water.

"Right, listen. When I let go, you can stand up. You won't reach for your knife, and you won't do anything stupid. Right?"

Tom nodded; it felt like his finger would break off if the man pushed any harder. He blessedly let go and stepped back. Tom took his finger in his hand and looked up, balefully. "What you go and do that for eh?" he moaned, "Could've broke me finger orf!"

The girl, who had been standing quietly on the gangplank, hopped lightly onto the deck and chimed in, "You shouldn't have gone for the knife, sir. We only want to chat. Walker's just a bit grumpy, on account of a bad sleep. You know how old men can be."

The man, Walker, grunted his response.

Tom struggled to his feet as George reappeared, chipped and cracked china tea cups clinking gently on a tray. "Here we go then," he burbled. "Got tea in the pot downstairs if anyone needs more, just ask." He beamed around at everyone.

The girl turned to him, "Thanks. George wasn't it?"

George nodded happily, setting the tray down onto an overturned shipping crate. "That's right miss, good guess! And what's your name?"

She smiled at him and retracted her visor. Tom saw her brown eyes, set above soft cheek bones and a curved jaw; below her thin lips sat a slightly proud chin. She would be quite pretty without the grime, he thought to himself.

"Daisy," she said. "Pleased to meet you." She held her hand out to George, who shook it heartily.

The girl turned to Tom, but Walker stepped between them. "Look," he said gruffly, "We can pay you. We need to get down the Avon, without going through the toll roads."

Tom glowered at him. "That would cost. What could you have that I want, Mister? You don't look like a man of much affluence."

He watched Walker look about, scanning the deck. He stroked his chin, thoughtfully. Tom could hear the rough bristles scratching along his finger. His gaze came to rest on the engine.

"See you got yourself an old petrol model there, Tom," he went on, "How do you keep her running?"

He looked back to Tom, who continued to scowl. "Can't run it. Don't take vegetable diesel. Last time we tried it just gurgled and did bugger all. So it's nothing more than a forty quid waste o' metal."

Walker grinned at him and took a satchel from his shoulder. It looked heavy, like a sack of rubble. As he rummaged, the girl helped herself to a cup of tea, thanking George. Tom stood there with his arms folded, until the man turned, with a rectangle in his hand.

"Here we are," he proclaimed, smiling winningly. "This book will teach you how to make the engine compatible with fuels made from vegetable oil." He held it out to Tom, who didn't take it.

"Can't read."

Walker's smile dimmed noticeably, much to Tom's secret pleasure; he wasn't lying, he really couldn't read.

"Unless it's got pictures and that in, it's worth diddly squat to me, chum. So unless you got—"

George interrupted, asking "Can I have a look please, Mister?"

The walker studied him, apparently noticing him for the first time. As George stepped up from the stairwell leading below decks, Tom noticed the walker take a step back. Yeah, he thought, that's right, your turn. But the man just smiled anew, and held the book out to George, who took it.

"Of course, who'd argue with a big Welsh fella like yourself?" he said.

George looked bashfully at the book, "Don't worry mister, I wouldn't hurt a fly really."

He opened the book, mouth working as he tried to read. The bloody great idiot, Tom thought, you can't read. If I can't read you definitely can't re—"

George looked over at him, as if he could read his mind, "I can read this Tom. No problem really. Few big words here and there, might be a few made up, looks a bit home-made, see, but I'm sure we'll work it out."

The giant smiled again and wandered back down the stairs, mumbling to himself about converter plates and ignition switches.

Tom stared at George as the realisation that the prior superiority he had always assumed he held waved rude signs in his face and laughed at him. He was suddenly acutely aware that his claim to captaincy may not be so infallible.

He swallowed and licked his lips as the man known as Walker ambled pleasantly over and smiled down at him. First George can read, and now this lanky bastard is smiling down at me, he thought? Why was everyone so damn tall? He folded his arms grumpily.

"Now then, Tom. I think that should grant us passage aboard your ship for now, right? Plus," and here he opened his cloak slightly, "You'll have two armed guards, free"

"But I wouldn't need guards if I wasn't goin' anywhere, you daft bastard! No chance," He shook his head, "I'll get that book back and you two can pis—"

Walker interrupted him by drawing a clinking pouch from his belt.

Tom eyed it as he bounced it in his hand. "I suppose I could take you along the river a ways."

Walker offered him the bag, and Tom took it hurriedly, before he could change his mind. "Where exactly are you going then, mister?"

Walker continued to look down at him, grinning humourlessly. "I'm afraid," he replied, "That we are going to the city."

19

Daisy sat on the side of the boat, which Tom had assured her was called either Port or Starboard, and watched the countryside stream past. She had managed to have a quick wash below decks, courtesy of George and his basin, and was feeling somewhat refreshed. Walker lounged against the thin mast, the sail of which was currently furled; the river's natural current was enough to carry them along for now.

George had taken the tea away and was currently doing things on deck, while Tom stood at the back steering the little boat behind the oversized steering wheel, which he claimed had come from an old 'pirate ship', like the ones she had read about. The river was smooth and wide enough that Tom had little steering to do, and the man was perched on a stool, flicking the wheel lazily.

She had never seen a boat, or a ship before in real life, and she had to admit she was fairly underwhelmed.

Tom's boat, and it was a boat, definitely not a ship, bobbed and churned along, its weathered pink hull radiating an almost apologetic sense of embarrassment. She had decided then that she would focus on their surroundings.

Daisy moved, sitting near the front of the boat, which Tom had insisted was the bow. She watched the scenery float past, oddly feeling that it was the world moving with the swells of the water and not herself and the boat.

They had gone past a field of huge windmills, slender and tall like fingers reaching skywards, some turning merrily in the wind, others sulking, still and silent.

Later they had come across a group of children playing on the bank, and some of the boys in the group had thrown stones, in the fair natured way of children that means no true malice. Tom had waved a pole at them, but they had merely laughed and resumed their games.

The Good Gel flowed along gently, passing various small villages and lonely buildings on the sides of the valley walls, dotted about high above and far away from them.

She was absentmindedly playing with her brother's old tag, when Tom shouted from behind her, "After this next bend, you should be able to see the city"

Daisy stirred; she'd never seen a city either. Her mother had worked there once, and had told her stories of their grandeur. She was excited, unlike Walker, who pulled his hat down over his face slightly and refused to turn to look. She found that she was holding her breath; after the disappointment of the 'ship', she was ready for huge buildings, gracing the sky with lights, bejewelled and glittering as her mother had told her. She had said it was busy, busier than the market back home, with people from all over the country. You could buy anything there, she had said, and the city never slept.

As the *Good Gel* crawled slowly around the bend in the river, she caught her first glimpse, off in the distance over the slopes of the hills ahead. She was not disappointed.

The ground towards the city was greener, with trees, tall and leafy. The sky around it seemed bluer, with more clouds than usual for the late autumn months. The river wound ahead of them, a blue scar through the green landscape, leading down and through the wall surrounding the city. Buildings were strewn sporadically along the roads leading there, becoming thicker and less spread out the closer to the city they got, until they stopped at the wall.

The wall itself was tall and grey, probably concrete, stretching high above the buildings that rested next to it. Vertical lines of blue intersected the grey mass, pulsing softly, as if the city was breathing. There were vast openings interspersed along the wall, tall dark arches cut into the concrete, which allowed the roads along the ground, as well as the river, to enter the city. The buildings beyond the wall raked the sky, punching into the clouds above.

But what struck Daisy most was the sheer activity bustling around the city. Through each of the arches streamed crowds of people like so many ants. Above the ants on the ground, ants patrolled along the top of the wall. Trucks, horse carts and boats all bustled along, coming and going along the roads and river way. Lonely looking petrol vehicles trundled along, causing people to spread as they rumbled through the masses. Above, distant birds of steel wheeled and dived, landing on or in the tallest buildings. She could hear the distant rumble of activity even here; the sound of thousands of people, living.

"Big, isn't it?"

Walker had appeared at her side. He glowered out at the city ahead. She didn't reply. She couldn't think of what to say. It was bigger than anything she had ever seen. The wall itself must have been a good twenty meters above the ground, and it was dwarfed by the buildings it enclosed. Her mother had sold the city short.

"It's... amazing" she managed.

Walker clucked and shook his head, "Thinking like that'll get you killed one day, girl."

He stalked back to his position at the mast, pointedly turning his back on their destination. He started to roll himself a cigarette as the girl joined him.

"And one day, those things are going to kill you," she replied.

He half shrugged and grunted.

"Why is the ground so much... greener here?"

He licked the edge of his roll, sealing it, before turning to look at her. "The city has its own weather patterns, girl. They make sure there's more rain, more cloud. Even though your town is only four days walk from here," he lit his cigarette, flicking the match overboard, "the weather patterns will be completely different."

She rubbed her head slightly, "How does that work? You can't just change the weather."

Walker looked up and gestured, "Know what a satellite is?"

She shook her head.

"Then you needn't worry about it. Just know it works." He exhaled and continued, "You ever seen snow? Real snow?"

Daisy thought back; she had only heard of snow from the old people living in her town, and even they only knew of it from relatives, or very young childhood memories. Supposedly it was cold, slow rain that could cause the entire country to close down, blocking roads with only the lightest of coverings. Daisy had always assumed it must be razor edged, and pitied the southerly countries she had been told about; the ones that apparently received vast amounts of this snow, almost constantly. She eventually shook her head,

"I've heard of it, but it's always so dry where I live..." her mind panged painfully back to her brother, and the home she no longer had, and she corrected herself, "...lived. And in the winter it's just icy and cold."

Walker scratched his chin, "Well, no matter. They have it here, but we won't see any. They try to emulate the weather as it was before the crisis, so they mainly keep it wet when it should be dry, and dry when it's too cold to enjoy." He shrugged and took another drag on his cigarette.

Daisy was confused, "Crisis? What do you mean? Hasn't it always been this way?"

Walker turned to her sharply. "You don't know about the crisis? Did your family not even try to teach you? Or are you just thick?"

Daisy scowled at him, "They taught me what they could. You know we didn't have books, or—"

George interrupted her. "Miss Daisy?"

With a final glower at Walker, she padded gently over to where he stood, on the bottom step leading below decks, as always.

"What's the matter, George?" she asked, smiling.

Daisy liked George. Always smiling, he radiated an almost childlike sense of goodwill, not seeming to judge anyone, seeing the good in them. He had failed to act when Walker had been threatening Tom, and was helpful and kind. But he was not childlike to look at. He was a giant of a man, taller than Walker by a good head and shoulders, with a shaved head and a huge, bushy black beard; like most overly-tall people, he stooped when standing next to others, or tried to stand so that he was more level with everyone else. His arms were solid, like roots of a tree, and his hands would easily have been able to enclose her head, and to squash it, if he'd felt like it. He made tea in slightly damaged china cups, sung heartily of his home country of Wales, and wielded the ten foot barge pole like she would a small stick.

He smiled hugely at her, white teeth gleaming through the forest of beard. He was still far taller than she was, despite the height difference in where they stood.

"I've noticed you playin' with that shiny tag; the one on your gun" he looked down at her softly, smiling, "I thought it must mean a lot to you, so I made you this, see?" He opened one huge palm and held out a leather strap.

"It isn't much," he conceded, "but it's the best I could do on this boat. It's a necklace, for the tag. In case you lose the gun, or something bad happens to it. Take it."

He grinned at her again, as she took the leather from him. It had a small clasp of rough, pewter coloured metal. She opened and closed it a few times. He saw her fiddle with it, and explained, "That's so you can add more things, if you want to, see?"

She smiled at him, "Thanks. It's a shame my brother isn't here, George."

George cocked his head slightly, still smiling gently at her. "Is it, Miss Daisy?"

"Yeah."

George held up a finger up gently, as though in thought. "We-ell, wherever he's gone, he's already gone there, right? So, if he was here, meeting me, he wouldn't have been able to do whatever it was that made you think of him so much, see? So, I reckon, the best thing to do is to let whatever he did help you to move on. Big things coming, could be. Everything that happens, happens because it has to, so that everything that has to happen after it can happen, see?"

She looked up at him. The beaming smile was still there, but there was a thoughtful twinkle in his eye.

"Come on," he continued, "I'll get you some more tea." He looked at her for a moment, then turned to go below deck. Daisy stopped him with a pat on the shoulder. He turned around, still grinning.

"Thank you." She whispered.

"No problem. No harm bein' nice, is there? " He ambled down to whatever was under the deck, radiating good natured stupidity. She headed back to Walker, who had been watching the whole thing.

"What did you do with that buffoon?" he asked.

"He's not a buffoon. You should talk to him, I think you'd be surprised."

He shook his head, muttering, as she knelt down and unholstered her gun. She held it upside down and, carefully, un-looped the chain holding her brother's tag to the grip.

55

She smelled, rather than felt, Walker looming behind her. "Try not to get sentimental, girl", he said, "Another thing that might kill you one day."

She ignored him and hooked the tag onto the leather necklace, placing it over her head and gripping the scratched metal tag, running a thumb over the pitted surface, feeling the beaming idiot's smile. She dropped it down the front of her jerkin.

The city was getting closer; the grass along the banks of the river was definitely greener, she could even see insects buzzing angrily away at their approach. The sky seemed even bluer than before and she could feel the sunlight warming her from above.

She smiled quietly to herself, as the boat continued its way gently through the water.

20

The afternoon sun sprinkled orange into the river as it descended sluggishly in the sky. Walker looked up at the water gate guiding the river into the city as Tom steered his boat slowly towards it. The traffic on the river was heavy. He kept the boat to the left, following the slow surge of watercraft. Walker checked ahead; the guards here were stopping boats, big and small, at random intervals, presumably to search for contraband.

He flicked the stub of his cigarette overboard and waved to the captain. "Are they likely to search this one, Tom?"

Tom scratched the light beard that peppered his chin, and shrugged. "They search everyone at some point Walker. You'll have to hope you have luck on your side."

He smiled unkindly and returned his attention to the river. Walker grunted and went down to find Daisy. She had gone below with George some time ago, probably for more tea. He would need her ready, should anything happen.

He headed down the narrow stairs and opened the door to the cabin below. It was dark, but felt comfortable. There was a lamp, swinging gently from the ceiling, throwing soft shadows around him. Walker could still smell the previous occupants of the hold, despite George's best efforts. He spotted a small counter, set up like a kitchen, where the china teaware clinked together softly with the swaying of the ship.

The girl and George were sat on a couple of the smaller crates, talking and looking at the book Walker had given the two men earlier.

"You need to come back up, girl," he said, "I need to keep an eye on you as we get into the city, make sure you don't do anything stupid."

She glared up at him, but remained seated. "Right, because you never do anything stupid."

Walker just looked at her. She stared back for as long as she could, but he was a seasoned scowler. She finally gave up and looked at the floor, reaching up to her visor and extending it to hide her eyes.

Walker nodded, "Just hurry up, you've got two minutes." He climbed the stairs back up, thinking to himself. The girl was getting braver; not necessarily a bad thing, but something he'd have to pay attention to. He could leave her in the city, he supposed. Plenty of traffic, she could even find a lift back to her home if she needed to.

She didn't seem to know anything at all about him, or the difference between Walkers and the Order; she didn't even know about the Crisis, so there'd be no problem leaving her here, alive.

Daisy appeared at his elbow, "I'm here, what do you need?"

He turned slightly towards her, rolling a cigarette. "Just be quiet and keep quiet. If they talk to you, I'll answer. Keep your visor down, it will help."

She nodded and ran a hand through her hair. Walker adjusted his shoulder bag, making it more visible, and moved his hat slightly further down his head, shading his face. The boat slipped slowly under the wall, through the concrete archway. They were cast in shadow, illuminated rhythmically every few seconds by the pulsing light coming from the cold blue glow of the glass strip running the length of the ceiling of the curved tunnel.

There were concrete jetties jutting from the tunnel's walls, running perpendicularly to each other each side of the tunnel just above the water level, where the guards stood, watching and calling people over. The guards ahead looked uninterestedly back at them but one, face unobscured, waved them over. Walker heard Tom mutter, but the boat slowly drifted towards the ledge to their left.

The officer held a glowing panel, which he swiped at with a gloved hand. He barked down at the passengers, "Climb over here, tie your vessel up."

Walker looked back towards Tom, who muttered again and clambered down from the steering platform, then scrambled over the side and dropped to the ledge. He watched as the officer and Tom spoke in low voices, waiting. The officer was shaking his head and looking towards Walker and Daisy. He pushed Tom aside and strode to the edge.

"You," he waved his pad at Walker, "What's in the bag?"

Walker hefted the bag and climbed onto the rail of Tom's boat. He stepped down easily onto the ledge and faced the officer. The pips on his shoulder indicated that he was a captain.

"Captain. You wouldn't want me to charge you with impeding the progress of a member of the Order, would you?"

The captain eyed him up, disdainfully.

"You, sir, are no member of the Order. You are dishevelled, dirty and, frankly," he sniffed, "Unwashed. What cohort did you pass out with?"

Walker replied immediately, "Tenth Cohort, Captain, the same one as your Commanding Officer, the Librarian." He took a step closer to the officer, who was the same height as he was. "And if you don't let me through now, *Captain*, I will be forced to report you to him. See how he likes it when a low ranking officer bothers him with matters suitable for, well, foot soldiers like you."

The man went paled. He looked levelly at Walker, just managing to keep face. "You are too young to..." The Captain trailed off, quailing under Walker's gaze. "Very well. Carry on." He went to turn, but Walker clamped a hand on his shoulder.

"Aren't we forgetting something, Captain?" The man glowered at him. His men were watching keenly, in the way that the lower paid ranks do when their superior is being made a fool of.

58

He snapped a salute, grudgingly, which Walker didn't return.

"Come on," he said to Tom, "Let's get a move on."

Tom hurried to untie them so they could leave, and jumped into the boat behind Walker.

"So you are in the Order? That means the book you gave us is legal, and everything? You're not one of them walkers then? 'Cos I thought, what with you giving that book away and all that y—"

Walker turned and grabbed him, and growled in a low voice, "If we are not moving within three seconds, that man is going to grow a set and search us properly. Move." He shoved Tom away.

As Tom hurried about, he turned and leaned against the mast, and placed his cigarette between his lips. He caught Daisy watching him, one eyebrow raised over her visor. He shrugged at her and lit up, inhaling deeply.

21

15 years ago...

Walker watched, grudgingly impressed, as the boy knocked all the cans down again. He turned to Walker , smiling arrogantly."Did it again, old man. I'd bet I'm a better shot than you."

He laughed out loud, remembering. He collected his gun from the boy and holstered it at his hip.

The lad watched him carefully. Nearly as tall as Walker now, he no longer had to crane his neck or stand on tip toes for them to be eye to eye.

He chuckled, shaking his head. "You have some way to go lad, before you're on par with me. Michael, though... "

"Michael?" he asked. "Who's Michael?"

Walker paused, reflecting. It couldn't hurt for the boy to know. He was 15, nearly a man grown. "He was... a friend. We trained together. In the Order."

The lad's eyes lit up, he always wanted to know more about the Order. He moved closer to Walker, and he noticed again the boy's size; far broader than he had been himself at that age. The lad would be big, bigger than Walker.

"That's when you trained as a philosopher, isn't it?"

Walker nodded. "Correct. He was a little younger than me, but as good as me in every respect, aside from shooting. Well," Walker added ruefully, removing his hat and scratching his dirty brown hair, "He was always better at close quarters than me. Could put you on your arse in three moves."

He laughed again at the memories, "Even though I was bigger than him. Every damned time."

The boy shook his head. "You didn't try hard enough, if a man smaller than you beat you in fighting. He should have been better at the learning, writing, and things like that."

Walker studied his young companion. He had the cocky headstrong sensibilities common in boys his age; an inconvenience few got over properly. He replaced his hat, and stepped towards his ward. "Why do you think that, lad?"

The boy scratched at the dusting of stubble on his chin. "Well, since you have the same training, and being of similar ages, you surely had the advantage. The size, the power. Brute strength. It doesn't make sense that a man, trained the same way as you, could beat you by being smaller and weaker."

Walker nodded; the boy had sound logic, but lacked tactical practice, as well as practical tactics; something easily remedied. "So, you think that power comes from size, brute force and sheer strength? Come then, a new lesson for you."

He turned away from the low wall of the farm the boy had been shooting at, and climbed easily over the battered fence that bordered the field behind them. The boy followed, vaulting the fence, landing next to Walker.

"So, you're going to teach me more moves?"

Walker shook his head. "No lad, you know all the moves. This is going to be about thinking."

The boy slumped his shoulders and moaned. "We already did my writing class today, I can read anything you show me, and I never mistake my grammar, unless trying to convince someone I'm a fool. What thinking can you teach me aside from that?"

Walker removed his hat and cloak, laying his book pack reverently upon the outstretched cloth, to protect it from the dust and grim of the field. He flexed, little pops answering from his chest; his armour needed a little work done, but the lifting plate at his back hissed coolly, still working fine. He grinned at the lad.

"Come, then. You're of a size that I can fight you and not worry about hurting you too much. Try and hit me."

The boy licked his lips hungrily. Walker noted, with some scorn, that the martial aspects of his training had always intrigued the boy more than the intellectual.

"You're sure?" the boy asked.

Before Walker could answer, the boy had lashed out, lightning fast, bringing his left arm close to Walker's face. Walker slipped sideways, to the boy's right, and tapped him in the gut, knocking the wind from him. The lad collapsed amongst the sparse weeds, spluttering.

"Good idea, trying to distract me. I thought you might," grinned Walker. "Come on, get up. That was a baby tap."

The boy clambered to his feet, glowering at Walker, who continued to grin amiably. He sprang toward Walker, feigning with his right and bringing a boot up towards Walker's groin. Again, Walker moved faster, palming the boot away, slapping the boy across the cheek, causing him to lose balance, and fall once again to the ground.

Walker laughed, sharply. "Boy, what happened? Come at me, properly, with all your strength. Show me what you—"

The boy launched himself at Walker, arms reaching up towards his throat. Walker grasped his arms and twisted himself down, as the boy rose over him. He flipped him easily on to the ground, where he proceeded to sit on him. The boy struggled underneath his weight, fruitlessly trying to wriggle free.

"Do you know why I won so easily, boy?" he asked pleasantly.

The boy, red faced and furious, spat curses up at his tormenter, as Walker rolled himself a cigarette. "You're bigger than me!" the boy growled, "And you know all the moves, you taught me them, for fuck's sake!"

Walker casually leant down and cuffed him roughly over the head. "Now, you know how I feel about swearing. No, you failed because you only used your strength, and then you got angry." Walker lit his roll up, and inhaled. "Whilst I, despite me clearly being stronger than you, used none against you. You need to think more, boy."

He treated the boy to another wallop about the head, before allowing the boy to catch his breath, and continued, "All I did was use your weaknesses. It's not enough to just go all out, all of the time. Strength will only take you so far. Much better to exploit an enemy's weaknesses. Which, if I'm honest, you had plenty of."

He chuckled and collected his hat and pack from the ground, before dusting off his cloak and fastening it beneath the clasp on his chest plate.

The lad turned angrily and stormed up to him, so they were face to face. "That's not fair! No wonder I lost."

Walker stared impassively back through his visor. "Think about it; I never said I wouldn't use your weaknesses. You knew that I'm bigger than you, and smarter than you. You did try a couple of clever tricks, of which I am impressed, slightly. But you got angry, and let me see every single move you would attempt. The flip," he exhaled, "Was all you."

The boy spluttered again, outraged, "But you're the teacher, how can that be fair?"

Walker ruffled his hair condescendingly, "What better way to teach than by example?" He called behind him as he strolled down the hill. "When you learn these lessons, and I hope you do, you'll be able to win. Think! Don't just act!"

The boy called back, "What kind of philosopher cheats, on purpose? A coward cheats. Real philosophers wouldn't have to cheat, or lie. They could just win."

Walker stopped and sighed. The boy had more to learn than he'd thought.

He turned to face the furious lad, "Why would a man, clever enough to outsmart his opponent, choose to waste time and energy on a 'victory' by any other means? I haven't been teaching you just to read books, boy. It's about reading people.

"A kind word here, a commanding voice there. It's about reading the situation. You wouldn't use a sledge hammer to repair a pistol, would you? Now come."

The boy came down the hill, sullenly, kicking at rocks and glaring at the floor.

Walker softened slightly. "If you learn these lessons properly, you may find yourself a place with the Order."

The boy's head shot up, "Really?"

Walkers' mouth smiled at him from below his visor. "Really." He lied.

22

Daisy's mouth fell open. When they had entered the tunnel the sun had been sinking, casting an orange glow from the horizon. She had expected it to be the dark of night on the other side, but she had come out blinking, mouth agape.

Everywhere seemed to be illuminated; there were lights on poles lining the streets, lights on buildings, twinkling in the sky high above them. Even the streets were glowing, with the same, rhythmic pulse that she had seen on the walls, and in the tunnel. The only lights they had had back home were lamps, usually paraffin, which eked a sullen amber glow that only darkened the shadows in the corners of rooms. Walker had begun to explain that the city used the sun and the river for power, but had lost interest, leaving it unfinished.

One of the birds she had seen earlier roared overhead and hovered. She could see that it was made of some kind of metal, as she'd thought, heat pouring from engines that glowed red. Walker looked up at it and pulled his hat down, hunching his shoulders away from the tunnel of wind being sent from its engines as it took off, wheeling away into the sky amongst the towering buildings above her.

He lurked a little way ahead of her now, furtively discussing something with a man wearing the strangest head gear she had ever seen.

One of the man's eyes was covered with what she could only imagine was glass. She could see writing pouring itself over the screen, then erasing itself as new writing appeared. The glass eye was attached, via a little arm, to a silver-blue band that went over the man's head from ear to ear. He noticed her watching, and glared at her.

"What are you staring at, huh?"

Daisy flicked her visor up, better to glare back at the little man, "Just admiring your headband."

The man spluttered indignantly, "It's not a headband, it's an optical input—"

Walker cut him off by gently slapping his cheek with one gauntleted hand. The man's scathing glower was replaced with an expression of mild shock, and he turned back to Walker. Eventually Walker straightened up, and gave the man some paper. He turned and scuttled away, peering back over his shoulder every now and then.

"Come on," he grunted.

They walked a little way before she asked him, "What treasure did you give him this time, then? More musical sheets? Or a recipe for really good alcohol made from, oh, I don't know, potatoes?"

He looked at her as they walked, and replied, "Vodka. It's called vodka."

She was confused. "What is? What you gave him?"

He stopped and laughed. "You really don't know anything, do you? Vodka is a drink."

Walker was making fun of her again. Annoyed, she started walking. He fell in beside her, and continued, "I gave him money. Old fashioned money."

She was curious, despite herself, "Paper money? Come on, be serious. How is it worth anything?"

He laughed again, "Very good question girl, how indeed?"

There it was again. The laugh. And he still wouldn't use her name. She seethed quietly. She would walk ahead, sod him. She looked around her as she stormed off, trying to forget him and taking in the sights. Everything in the city was amazing, outweighing her annoyance, but she was already becoming quite overwhelmed.

The brightness was no longer causing her to squint at everything, but the noise was deafening. There seemed to be people everywhere, casting a deafening umbrella of noise around them like some horrible weapon. Food stall owners bellowed about their wares as people walked to and fro, jostling one another and arguing. A sudden gust of laughter drew her attention, and she found herself looking into an inn, full to bursting with drinkers.

A drinking establishment full with drinkers is not in itself an odd thing, but Daisy found herself perplexed by the sight before her.

She could see straight in to the inn, as if there were no walls. Lights shone sharply at random intervals, floating unexplained in front of the patrons, none of whom seemed the slightest bit worried. She walked towards the room, watching bemused as the lights danced and played.

There was a finely carved bar of wood, a man stood behind it pouring softly coloured drinks into elegant, intricate glasses. The customers laughed, sipping and smiling. Daisy stepped closer, meaning to further examine the clothes they wore in the city and—

There was a crack as Daisy hit her head, knocking her back, where she bumped heavily into a man hurrying behind her.

"Watch it, you idiot!" he cursed, pushing her away and hurrying on again.

It was glass! The inn was made of glass! And she had walked headfirst into it. The people inside were now laughing at her; she spun away into the crowd, face reddening. She flicked her visor down, to hide from their leering faces.

Her face continued to bloom red, her cheeks flushing with hot shame as she pushed through the crush of people.

The floating lights had been reflections. She'd seen glass before, and it was practically everywhere in this place. Even the people had glass, in their visors, on those little eyes-on-a-stick headbands she had seen. She was furious at herself. An idiot, clumsy, stupid...

Lost.

Walker had obviously carried on, oblivious, or uncaring. She looked about, panicking. How could he leave her? What would she do now? She knew no one! Daisy looked about her, at the people as they streamed past. None of them looked particularly helpful. Someone bumped into her.

"Hey, watch wh—"she got bumped again, and nearly fell. Daisy looked about desperately, seeking refuge.

She finally found something, an opening between the buildings. She pushed and squirmed her way towards the darkness of the alley, eventually bursting free of the crowd, half running, half falling to freedom.

She stood, slowly getting her breath back. Okay, she thought, don't panic. Just think like Walker.
She stopped. She realised she didn't know how to think like him; she didn't actually *know* the man at all. Panic threatened to overwhelm her, when a voice skulked from the shadows behind.

"When you don't know where you're going, can you still get lost?"

She wheeled about, and saw nothing. There was a rattle further down the alley, but it was too dark for her to see anything; in this city of lights it was just her luck to find the only bloody dark spot.

"If a ship has no destination..." drawled the voice, "Then no wind is favourable".

Stay calm, she thought. "Come out then," she said aloud. Her voice sounded empty and high against the rumble of the city behind her.

Silence.

She swallowed, and took a breath, stilling her nerves. "I am a bit lost, actually," she conceded.

There was a grating noise from the dark that could've been a chuckle. A large, smooth egg appeared slowly from the gloom. The egg appeared to be wearing a visor, much like hers, and seemed to be attached to a neck. The rest of the man appeared, and Daisy took a step back.

It wasn't that the man was deformed; he was viciously skeletal; his ribs stuck out painfully, marked sharply by the faded baby blue body suit hanging about his gaunt frame. His head, looking all the more massive due to the thinness of his body, was almost entirely encased in a helmet of some sort, with only his mouth and jaw extending pointedly from the curved helmet. The visor was thick and stood out from the helmet by some way, and was jet black. Daisy found herself wondering how the man could see, when he spoke.

"A lost little flower in the grime of the big city. Do you know what a cliché is?"

Daisy was confused. He sounded less hoarse than before, and happier. "What are you talking about?"

The helmet ignored her, and a long, thin arm rose, waggling a bony finger at her. "You know not the danger you place yourself in. Such a silly child."

He grated again, Daisy felt sure she saw dust come from the creature's mouth. "Hey, watch your tone," Daisy said, indignation overriding her confusion and fear. "Who do you think you are anyw—"

This time he broke in, mewling forlornly again like he had when he first spied her from the shadows.

"Forgive me. My reality becomes... confused at times. It's the helmet, gone a bit funny."

She heard the grating noise again. He must be coughing. No one laughs like that.

Daisy ran her hands through her hair. "Okay, don't worry. Look, I'm lost; I need to know where someone would go, to look for..."

She trailed off, she still didn't know what they were doing out here, in the city. The man interrupted.

"Look, come here and help me. I can't reach round the helmet here; I'm so addled and fuddled."

He held his hands out, imploring and pathetic, "There's a switch, at the back; should help with my... problems" The last word blurted out, as though it had been difficult for him to say.

She eyed him carefully, knowing she had little choice but to do as this horrible thing said. She couldn't go into the street; no one would even look at her, let alone tell her where she had to go. She moved closer to him.

"Oh, thank you miss, you won't regret it. Ole Rifty'll have something nice for you, after"

She stopped. That didn't sound quite right. "What do you mean?"

The man didn't reply. She stepped back, watching him. The man had gone quite still. She waved a hand in front of his visor. Drool was coming from one corner of his mouth.

"Hey? Hello?" she groaned. "Don't be dead," she pleaded, "I need to find out where—"

There was a dry, familiar chuckle from behind her. "He's gone, girl."

She spun around as Walker strolled down the alleyway towards her. "Walker! Thank God!"

He smirked at her, then bent to examine the old man. "Do you even know who God was?"

She ignored him. "Where did you go? You just left me, I could've—"

He looked at her sharply, "Stop," he warned. "Just pay attention next time." He paused, smirking, "How's your head?"

She blushed, all praise and thanks forgotten. She scowled at the back of his head as he clucked disapprovingly and prodded the man, who stayed stiff as a board and toppled ponderously backwards.

Walker straightened up, seemingly satisfied. "Come on then. We've got to get moving, we're meeting someone."

He strode past her out of the alley and turned left. She hurried to keep up as they merged once again with the faceless, laughing crowds of the city.

23

As Walker stalked through the crowd, shoving and bumping people out of the way, he could feel his mood sinking. No respect in the cities, he thought to himself. A man stopped directly in front of him; Walker didn't slow, and knocked the man out of the way.

"Hey, fuck nut, watch it!" the man yelled.

Walker ignored him and continued on his way, Daisy scurrying along in the wake he made through the crush of people.

She called out from behind him. "Why are there so many people out at this time? Don't they sleep?"

Walker ignored her too. Trying to talk over the dull roar of the city would be a waste of effort. He couldn't even roll himself a smoke. He scowled about him, looking for the pink and orange glow of Charlie's bar. He started to head towards the lights ahead, when he heard the girl cry out again.

He turned to see her wrestling a man, who had grabbed at the money pouch on her belt. He sighed and went to step over, but stopped, surprised. He grinned to himself as the man wheezed, bent double. The girl withdraw her knee from his groin, before swinging her arm wide, knocking the man out cold with a blow to his temple.

Walker chuckled and strode over as people watched. Daisy shook her hand and looked down at the crumpled heap that had tried to rob her.

"Nice punch." He said, calmly.

"Never punched someone from a city before." She blew on her knuckles.

Walker chuckled and grinned at her. "More satisfying, right?"

67

She shrugged, "Hurts just the same."

He stooped and briefly leafed through the man's pockets; some coins, paper money, probably from previous victims, and some tobacco. He pocketed the tobacco, grabbed the money and straightened up.

"Good pay for good work." He handed the girl the money.

"Where did you learn to fight like that, girl?" He glanced back at the moaning figure on the pavement behind them. "Groin shot like that, some might call that cheating."

She glanced back at the man lying prone on the ground and shrugged. "Cheating is what the losers call it. Not really cheating if you're fighting to win."

Walker grunted as they strolled through the surging crowds. "Where did you learn that?"

She ran a hand through her hair, pushing it back from her visor. "I didn't. Better to be smart, think a little."

He scowled behind his visor and sped up slightly, "Keep up. Nearly there."

The club was an old building near the centre of the city. In past times is had been used as a sort of indoor arena for performances; actors and musicians would play here for the city, and before even then the building had once been used to showcase exotic animals. Now the building was mostly unused, boarded off. The only areas open were the lobby area which was now the main bar, and the backstage areas used by the bar staff.

From the street, the building looked out of place. Old stone stairs led from the newer, gleaming pavement up to large double doors, painted a red that shone darkly in the street lights. It squatted grimly between the modern sky scrapers that flanked it, ageing grey columns and buttresses shown in all their decrepit glory by the floodlights installed on the balcony overhead.

Walker glared up at it, the sinking feeling returning. He didn't like Charlie, but he was the best man to get information from, without asking any questions of his own. He began to head up the steps, but paused.

He turned to Daisy. "Girl, you must keep your head down in here. He's tricky. Remember, be clever. Think a little."

The bouncers watched him come. They were big men, in big suits designed to make them look dangerous, but in a civilised, controlled way. They eyed him suspiciously. Having been instructed to 'use their better judgment' when it came to letting people in to the club these days, they had found their job decidedly harder. However, they knew that for someone to be allowed in, they shouldn't look dangerous, or be armed, or look like they had been sleeping in the same clothes for several weeks.

The man approaching now, smiling up at them like a fox amongst hens, was all of these things, as was the girl behind him. Both looked dangerous, were fairly dirty and were definitely armed. The man was even holding his cloak aside, for them to get a better view.

He was a definite no-no on the bouncer's mental entry-or-not-checklist. The more diplomatic, quicker thinking of the two bouncers stepped forward, genially blocking Walker's path.

"Sorry sir, the club is at full capacity," he lied, "We've been told to stop allowing entry tonight. Please come back tomorrow." He smiled down at Walker in what he hoped was a disarming way.

Although the man was smaller than him, the bouncer didn't feel like getting into a fight with him. He got paid to push about the non-dangerous, smaller-than-himself kind of person, who had had too much drink or too many drugs; people who wouldn't fight back even if they were in any state to.

His attempt at a smile melted, as the man in the hat continued to smirk up at him. It was very disconcerting, he realised, not being able to see people's eyes. He looked past the man to the girl who was rubbing her head slightly. She was also wearing a visor. The two of them in visors, the gun at the man's hip. The light bulb of slowed understanding finally clicked on in the man's head.

The bouncer hurriedly stepped back, and clicked a button on his ear piece. "Hey, it's Rob. Tell Charlie there's a... the walker, he's out here."

Walker beamed at him. "I knew you'd get there eventually." He stepped forward, pausing to pat the man on the arm as he went.

"Well done."

24

The doors closed behind them as Daisy and Walker entered the bar. She flicked her visor up and stared, open mouthed, at the sheer activity in front of her. The ceiling hung low, but the room felt immediately large and very busy. Tables and chairs were everywhere, except for a wide area of floor, near the back of the smoky room, where people were dancing to the music.

Daisy had never heard anything like it in her life. It was... basically noise, but rhythmic, tribal, rising from the floor and shaking your bones. It made you want to move, shake your arms, kick your legs and jump about. She found herself nodding along with the beat.

The room was lit, but in a strange, dark way, and coloured lights shone and spun through the smoky air, twisting with the music. Sullen grey clouds billowed from somewhere, wreathing the dancers in a strange mist. She began to panic, telling Walker that the building must be on fire. He waved a hand dismissively, assuring her it was false, made by a machine. Everything here was new and strange.

"I think I need a drink." She murmured.

Walker cupped his hand to his ear and shook his head, indicating he couldn't hear her. He leaned closer and bellowed in her ear. "I NEED A DRINK."

He walked towards the bar and pushed through the crowd of people clamouring to be served. He shouldered his way to a spot at the bar, and motioned for her to join him. People would shoot argumentative looks, but noticed the casual way Walker had his pistol on display, a clear warning to even the most flash addled mind. The waitress came, and Walker ordered two whiskeys, neat.

Daisy turned to look out at the club again. On the far side of the room were some comfortable looking booths, partitioned for privacy, where people lounged, smoking, laughing and drinking. The waitress returned with their drinks, which Daisy accepted gratefully. She sipped and was surprised; it was smooth and warm, not like the rough sawdust drink she was used to. She sipped again and turned to Walker, leaning in so she could hear him.

"What are we doing in here, then?"

He downed his drink and grunted. "I need to see someone about a book."

"A book? Which one?"

He turned to the barmaid, pointing to his glass and signalling for another. "It's not important, girl. Just keep an eye out for him."

Daisy looked at him. "How am I supposed to find him if I don't even know—"

Someone tapped Walker on the shoulder, and the two of them turned. A slender woman, all shadowed curves and gleaming cheek bones, stood unsmilingly behind them.

"Mister Charles asks that the two of you," she eyed them disdainfully, wrinkling her nose at them. "Wait for him in the booths over there." She waved an arm to the far wall. "A booth has been set aside for you, and a waiter will be on call for drinks, which are on the house."

Again, she wrinkled her nose, sneering at the unsavoury idea of the two of them drinking for free. "If you'd like to follow me."

She turned gracefully, the crowd parting around her slender frame. Daisy glanced at Walker, who shrugged and grabbed his fresh drink.

"Come on. Might as well get comfortable."

Daisy took her drink and followed the two of them.

25

Walker sat at the shadowy booth and motioned for Daisy to join him. She sat on the red leather and marvelled at how soft it felt. She leaned back, looking on as Walker rolled himself a cigarette, sipping her fresh glass of whiskey the waiter had brought. She began watching the dancers to her right, twisting and jerking with the thumping bass.

Walker drummed his fingers on the table, impatiently. He had drunk his whiskey in one and now he scowled around the room, his normally easy smile replaced with a thin lipped frown.

"So, who's this Mr Charles?" she asked.

Walker's fingers continued their rhythmic drumming. "An old contact of mine. Charlie."

Daisy nodded and sipped at her drink, "You don't like him?"

Walker stopped drumming the table and looked at her sharply. He stayed quiet for some time, then agreed. "Not a lot, girl. Very astute of you."

Daisy couldn't tell if he was being sarcastic or not, but left it. "What are we doing here, then?" she asked.

His fingers began their tapping anew, the staccato beat rumbled on the table, and up Daisy's arm. "Asking a lot of questions, aren't we?"

Daisy shrugged at him, "Well, I've come this far. I just want to know what we're doing here."

Walker shrugged back, "Fair enough. Charlie sells things. I need something specific from him."

Daisy swirled her drink, watching the smoky liquid as it nearly spilled over the edges. "So why have you only just come here?"

Walker looked out over to the dance floor, where the people were still stomping and twirling to the music.

Daisy pressed on, "I mean, if you've been wandering around, looking for something specific, why only come to Charlie now?"

Walker turned his gaze back to Daisy, "The country is a big place, girl. It takes a long time for anyone to get anywhere. And," he paused, still tapping, "When it takes so long to get anywhere, or do anything, you have to be sure of what you are doing."

She mulled this over in her head, "You don't trust him?"

Walker grunted and turned towards her. As always, his eyes were hidden, but his mouth twisted unpleasantly. "Hard to trust something like that, lass"

She frowned, puzzled, "What do you mean, that?" But she was interrupted by Charlie's arrival.

He was short, probably shorter than she was, but wide. His shoulders indicated that, at some point, he'd been in fine physical shape. His chest was still wide and powerful looking, but he had the middle stages of a beer belly which, oddly, suited him; he was dressed smartly in an old fashioned pinstriped suit, cleverly stitched to make his stomach seem impressive instead of just fat. He wore dark glasses, but she could make out twinkly mischievous eyes through the dark plastic.

"Alright my son," He began, in an accent she didn't recognise.

He extended his hand towards Walker, who ignored it. He shrugged, turned to Daisy and lifted his glasses. He flashed a sly smile and winked at her. She felt a quick heat flush at her cheeks and wished she hadn't drunk her whiskey so quickly. She flicked her visor down, so Charlie couldn't see her eyes, and he laughed.

"Don't worry bird," Charlie crowed, "You ain't my type" He winked again, "Scoot then, scoot!" he waved his arms at her, indicating she should move up.

He squeezed himself into the curved booth, stomach resting gently against the table. He waved to a waiter and held up three fingers. The man nodded and headed to the bar. Daisy peered closer at Charlie. Something about him felt... off.

He had a cool, disarming charm, certainly, and his mannerisms seemed right. But there was something about his eyes; they were too bright, and his skin was just a little too shiny. The strobing lights in the club made everyone's skin flash and change unnaturally, changing even the most beautiful faces into waxy, leering masks, but the way his bald head gleamed reminded her of a silver moon.

"Back again I see, my son. Enjoying your stay?" he nodded to Walker, who scowled back.

"You know I hate the city, Charlie. I came to ask some questions. I assume you still deal?"

Charlie smiled winningly, as the waiter brought them fresh drinks. He picked his colourful glass up. It had a pink umbrella, with what looked like a little green bird on a stick floating in it. He sipped through the straw, his pudgy little finger sticking out daintily.

Smacking his lips appreciatively, he replied, "Now, now, now, Richard, not even a hello?"

Daisy glanced at Walker; the fingers on his left hand had twitched at the name.

" What a way to treat a long lost mate!"

He turned to Daisy, who was holding her fresh glass loosely; it smelled strongly of liquorice. "That's old Walker for you though, innit? That's sambuca, by the way. Put 'airs on your chest, just what a young lady like yourself wants, eh?" He laughed loudly and sipped at his drink again. "Now," he continued, placing his drink carefully on a fresh beer mat. "You know full well what I do, son. Finest purveyor of goods this side of anywhere."

Walker grunted again and downed his drink. He still looked uncomfortable, refusing to sit back in the booth seats.

Daisy sniffed at her drink, as Charlie carried on, "I'm a club owner, and proprietor of entertaining peoples and acts, all legal and above board. The boys in black even come down here, now and again. None tonight. Yet. Lucky for you"

He laughed again, as Walker leaned forward. Daisy could feel the anger pouring off of him.

"Careful, *mate*" Walker growled, "Not in front of the girl."

Daisy bristled slightly. She went to speak, but Charlie interrupted by standing suddenly. He leant his knuckles on the table and his voice took on a darker, nastier tone.

"Listen up, *sunshine*," he snarled. "You ain't the big man in these parts. You're all alone. And that means I 'old all the cards, see? So you mind your manners while we do business an' I won't call your old mucker down from on high, alright?"

He reached in to his suit and produced a cigar, long and thin. He lit it, drawing deeply and exhaled vile smelling smoke. Daisy struggled not to cough, wafting the smoke from her face. Even with the visor down, it stung her eyes.

Walker didn't react. Charlie grinned nastily. "So," Charlie said, smoothing his suit and sitting himself back down. He leaned back in the booth, cigar in hand, his previous cheeky smile again on his face. "Not told her who you are then, mate?" He raised an eyebrow, stirring his drink with the bird on a stick, "Best mind what I say then, hadn't I?"

Walker remained still and quiet, which worried Daisy. She watched the two of them carefully.

"So," Charlie carried on, turning his gaze from Walker to Daisy, "who've you brought along this time?" He exhaled again, and this time she couldn't help it; she coughed.

"Aw, I'm sorry" he said, theatrically waving at the air. "I'll put this out for now".

He leaned forward and dropped the cigar into the ice at the bottom of his glass. Daisy was about to reply, when he suddenly darted forward and grabbed her by the chin. She gasped as he retracted her visor. He pulled her forward, so that they were almost nose to nose. She struggled to free herself, as his eyes shone into hers.

"Let go!" she cried, grabbed his arm; it felt hard through the suit's material.

"A nice young filly you got yourself here, Walker" Charlie said, still staring into her eyes. He laughed, but with no humour.

"Probably about twenty years. Not chipped, so from, oh, out there somewhere," He waved vaguely with his free hand, smirking at Walker, "Like the last one. That boy."

Daisy looked back into Charlie's eyes; they were too bright, the wrong way round, like little lights in pools of darkness; his pupils glowed of their own accord. She battered her free hand against his chest, totally unnoticed by Charlie. She swivelled her eyes madly towards Walker, noticed he had bristled, but hadn't moved to help.

Her breath started to quicken; Walker was not going to help her.

Charlie leered at her. "Wonder how long this'un'll last for then? Oh?"He stopped leering and looked down. Daisy had her gun pressed firmly against his ribs. Charlie chuckled and carefully let go of her face.

"No need for that, young lady. Was just checking who you are." He waggled an eyebrow at her as she glared up at him. "Put it away nice and slow, and I'll get us a drink, shall I?"

He smiled and sat back as Daisy removed her gun, rubbing at her chin. Charlie stuck a hand in the air and, again as if by magic, a waiter came over.

"Summink fruity for me, mate, and whatever these two want. Whiskey? Cider? Eh?"

When Walker and Daisy ignored him, he turned to the waiter, "Best make it a whiskey each, son." The waiter nodded and moved off, as Daisy shuffled away from him.

"What's your name then, missy?" he asked her, as if nothing had just happened.

Daisy looked at him, nonplussed, eyes still watering. His grip really had been strong. "Why would I tell you anything? You're lucky I don't shoot you, never mind him!"

She glanced at Walker, who merely shrugged.

"Now, now, don't get arsey on me love," he said, as the waiter returned with their drinks. Charlie's eyes gleamed happily at the new drink in front of him, which was even brighter and more garish than the last. "No harm done and all that, just needed to see who you are," He sniffed his drink and stirred it with a new plastic stirrer, which had a bright red dog on the top "Or who you were."

74

He shot her a fresh grin and drank. The sugar from the rim of the glass coated his lips. She scowled at the man in front of her.

"It's Daisy," she spat.

Charlie nodded. "Nice name love, nice name. Don't get many daisies growing these days, but you've done alright."

"What did you mean by chipped?" she asked. She had never heard the word before, except when talking about potatoes.

Charlie pursed his lips and placed his drink down. "Oh, just the term we use for inner-city types, might come in here looking to trick ole Charlie. But you're alright, not a bug in you."

Daisy opened her mouth but Walker interrupted again. She scowled at him. "Enough games, Charlie. I've come here to ask a favour."

Charlie raised an eyebrow and looked back to Walker, sipping at his cocktail. "A favour he says?"

He put down his drink and licked the sugar crust from around his mouth, making a smacking noise."That's fine, me old mucker, ask away!" He grinned his boyish, happy grin, as Daisy rubbed at her face.

As Walker opened his mouth to speak, Charlie interrupted, "But you gotta do me one first, alright?"

Walker closed his mouth and resumed his scowl, as Charlie continued. "There's this guy, needs a helpin' hand, sort of thing. He's one of those junkies, addicted to the VR helmets, I'm doin' me bit as a member of the community and all that. All you gotta do is take him some cash. Easy, right?"

Daisy broke in, despite herself, "VR? What does that mean?"

"Virtual Reality." Walker grunted, "Like the man you met in the alley. Be quiet, girl."

Daisy glared at him again, and flicked her visor back down. She knew he did it on purpose, but it still annoyed her.

Charlie took a noisy slurp of his drink and sighed happily. "Bloody lovely stuff, this; you should try it. Synthesised fruit juice, o' course, can't grow the pomegranates 'round here." He took another drink, and turned to Daisy again, who flinched slightly.

"Virtual Reality Helmet, takes 'em to a new place. Only in their 'eads, o' course. Some daft buggers get lost in there though. Big ole place, the human mind. No truck with it meself." He chuckled and turned back to Walker. "The bloke ain't dangerous, so don't gotta worry about that. He'll see those big ole blasters you two brought in here, you cheeky sods, and probably shit his pants. Oops!" He stopped and placed a hand theatrically over his mouth, "Slip o' the tongue, Daisy, I do apologise. Such language in front of a lady."

It was her turn to scowl; she could see why Walker didn't like this grinning idiot. "Fuck this. I'm going to the bar."

Charlie laughed, clapping, while Walker watched moodily. "Got a temper on her, Walker. I like a bit o' fire in a lady!"

As she got up, she purposefully bumped the table, spilling Charlie's drink. He stopped laughing, and she turned to him with her hand placed over her mouth. "Oh dear," she cried in mock sorrow, "I've spilled your drink and now your suit's wet. Such a shame!"

She thought he would react badly, maybe threaten her, give her a chance to get even for his rough hands earlier, but he merely laughed, harder.

"That's alright gal," he chortled. "You go over to the bar and wait for the adults to be finished. I'll see to it the boys serve you, free o' charge." He winked, grinning and turned back to Walker, who hadn't moved.

Daisy stood there, looking at the back of his head shining in the light. The man was insufferable! And Walker did nothing. Not that she really expected him to. She rubbed at her chin and stalked off through the club towards the bar, knocking one drunken man over and taking a drink from another.

26

When Daisy was out of sight, Charlie's grin faded.

"You're gonna get her killed, mate." He sipped at his drink, eyes twinkling form behind his dark glasses. "Remember the last one?"

Walker's mouth darkened further. "Let's not, okay? Besides," he said, looking over to where Daisy stood arguing with someone at the bar, "She can look after herself."

"Well," Charlie replied, sipping thoughtfully at his cocktail, "The last one could look after himself, if I remember rightly, be a shame to see another one..." Charlie made a gun shape with his hand and held it against his head, blowing a raspberry loudly.

Walker glowered at him. Charlie shrugged and put his glass down.

"Just play it safe mate. Head down, all that. The less publicity, the better." He cocked a thumb to where Daisy had finished her argument with a decisive kick. "Now," he continued, "To the job."

"You want me to kill him, then?" Walker replied.

Charlie looked genuinely surprised, and shook his head. "So quick to jump to that, mate? I only want you to meet the poor bastard."

He leaned in conspiratorially. "He and I have this deal going on, see; he says he knows the best ways to get stuff into the city, and all that. Says he knows the big boys—"

Walker interrupted. "Less story, Charlie. Just tell me what you need me to do."

Charlie sat back and pulled a small, brass cigar case from his breast pocket. He clicked it open and took out a fresh cigar. He lit it with a match and puffed heartily, before closing the lid again.

"He's a weird fella, thinks too much. Been stuck in the VR for, well, ages. But he knows people, gets good stuff in, Flash, Juice... He also knows where to get hardware, if you need anything like that." His eyes glittered meaningfully, as Walker shrugged.

Charlie nodded and flipped his cigar case over. He pressed a switch along the side and the back flickered into life. Walker saw a familiar egg shape, and faded blue clothing.

"Funny. I've already met him tonight."

Charlie nodded, flicking his cigar ash into Daisy's abandoned drink, which flared briefly as the spirits were set alight. "Hilarious, I'm sure. Just remember, he's a bit weird. Jumpy. So watch yerself. Here's the dough." He slid a small satchel over to Walker. It clinked heavily as he took it. "Still," Charlie continued, "he gets the good shit. Valuable, he is. Meet him in the alley next to the Window Bar; you probably saw it on your way here?"

Walker smirked humourlessly. "Yeah, we saw it. I'll be back in an hour."

"Just tell him ole Charlie sent you."

Walker finished his drink and left the booth, leaving Charlie smoking his cigar.

Daisy had just finished downing another whiskey when Walker appeared behind her. She spun, furious.

"I told you, I'm not dancing witchu" she looked up at Walker, slightly unsteady. "Oh, it's you. We goin' now?"

She's drunk, he thought. He peered down at the last man who had bothered Daisy, still writhing slowly on the ground. "I see you've been practising. I'm off out. I'll be back soon."

She glowered up at him, wobbling slightly. "Well, tha's fine. I'll stay here an' drink, on my own. 'S'not like you'll need help out there, or anything." She added sarcastically.

Walker shook his head disapprovingly and scratched his chin. "Just stay here, girl," she scowled harder at him, "I've got some business to take care of."

"'Ere, you stop calling me—"

Walker ignored her, and headed out.

27

14 years ago

The boy watched impassively as Walker addressed his followers, remembering his words.

"Keep calm, stay quiet, and *pay attention*,"

They had headed into the city, to a bar. The boy had been amazed by the lights, the machines; the sheer volume of people. Walker had headed to a place owned by a man named Charlie, whom the boy disliked.

Charlie was too smiley, always grinning annoyingly. His skin was waxy, and his eyes shone too brightly, little flashes of blue behind darkened glasses. Walker had told him what the 'man' was, and the boy distrusted 'him' entirely.

Charlie stood away from the group of walkers watching, bright sugary drink in hand.

"We are at risk, my friends. Mother is sending the Order after us, trying to stop our mission."

There were murmurs from the crowd, as Walker continued. "The walkers are now outlaws, and we are in danger. We have to tread lightly, and take care."

A woman in the group stood up. She had dyed green hair, almost entirely hidden beneath an old style bowler hat, and she wore an old waistcoat under her russet hued duster. As she stood, she leaned on a large rifle, heavy looking, with a scope that glittered a green hue whenever it moved. She was a sniper, the boy noted with some cognizance; despite her weapon being almost as tall as she was, she held it with a strange fondness, her movements spoke of fluidity; strong and fixed, but nevertheless graceful.

"So, Walker, what are we going to do?" she gestured to the gathering around her. "This is all of us; we can't start fighting back. We're out here, being hunted like animals. Maybe it's time to stop this shit, end what we're doing!"

There were some sounds of agreement from those around her. Walker held up a placating hand, but the woman didn't sit. The boy ground his teeth.

"Ivy, be calm. We cannot fight them, true. But we must carry on our mission. Father would have wanted it. He would have demanded it. The Order has betrayed his teachings, and Mother leads them to folly, and ruin. Our goal is to finish what Father started; to gather knowledge, to keep it safe from the vulgar people who would waste the gift."

The woman known as Ivy shook her head and retracted her slim, pale green visor. Her deep blue eyes stared quizzically up at Walker. "And so what? What does this mean? We can't stay in the cities anymore. Not here, especially. Didn't you hear? Michael is here. Looking for us."

There was a moment of stillness; the boy noticed Walker's jaw muscles tensing. "Michael..." he began, "Is a problem. You're right. We can't stay in the cities. Especially not here." He sighed and rubbed at his chin.

"We have to separate, scatter around the country. Do what we can until such a time as we can take the Order back."

Ivy opened her mouth to speak, but was interrupted by a deep voice from the back of the room.

"Why wait, Walker? Could we not take Mother by force?" A huge bear of a man rose to his feet ponderously. His teeth shone brightly from between dark lips, his eyes hidden behind a softly gleaming visor. He had no hat, and his hair was swept back in knots, running down his back. His coat was heavy looking and dark.

Ivy turned to him incredulously. "By force? Look at us Idris! There must be thirty walkers in this room, and that's all of us. No one else from our cohort will join us, and the new recruits are already being trained to hunt us down!"

The big man known as Idris looked solemnly first at her, then Walker. "Walker, I say we go for Mother. Small groups can operate secretly, under cover. There's no way we could storm the Order head on. This is true. A small team though, four or so of us, the best of us, we could sneak in, take her out. Re-establish the Order's true purpose."

He stood, watching Walker carefully. Walker rubbed his chin again, a habit he had picked up from the boy, and thought. He reached into his cloak and withdrew his tobacco pouch, slowly rolling himself a cigarette.

"Where is Mother, Idris? No one has seen her since we left the academy, when we became walkers. No one knows where she went, who is guarding her," he smiled wanly, "Unless you've developed psychic powers overnight."

There was a chuckle from the crowd, as Idris looked coolly back at him. "Looks like the Walker is afraid. When did you lose your courage, man?"

That was too much; the boy started forward. "You mind your tongue, bastard!" He reached Walker's side, but was stopped by his outstretched arm.

Idris laughed, his voice cannoning around the room. The boy could feel it reverberate in his chest. "Look, the great Walker has children fighting for him now. Hey," he chuckled, looking around the room, "Perhaps we should have this young pup lead us? He's certainly got the fire for it!"

"Put it away, boy." Walker murmured quietly. "Let me deal with this." To Idris he said, "You would lead the Walkers then, Idris? Into the jaws of hell and back? Overthrow Mother and bring about a new golden age for the Order?

"And why now? Why would it make sense for us to rise up and fight Mother now, rather than before, or later? Surely it would have been obvious to any of us when, if ever, it would have been a good idea to attack?" He chuckled slightly, and Idris' hands clenched into fists. Walker continued.

"Hands up, those amongst you who would gladly follow this man?"

The group remained still, and silent. Ivy was still standing, watching the exchange between the two men.

"What makes you so special?" Idris growled.

Walker laughed again, "Come now, Idris. We're all friends here." He began to make his way through the group towards Idris. When he reached him, he stood there, looking up. The man was easily a foot and a half taller than Walker, and he towered darkly above him. The boy slowly unclasped his holster, just to be sure.

Walker spoke to the man, so quietly that no one could hear. The boy watched, aware, waiting for him the attack, but Idris just stood there. He turned his head away, and spoke.

"No."

He turned from Walker and stormed out of the room, flinging a chair from his path. As the door slammed behind him, Walker spoke to the group.

"Idris has gone for some fresh air."

He made his way back to the front of the room and turned back to the group. "Despite what some of you think, killing Mother would not help our cause. In fact, if Mother were violently removed, the current cohorts would rise up, led by our old associates, and wipe us out. For now," he took a drag on his cigarette, "We are relatively safe. I know we're being hunted, but only for our books."

He turned to Ivy, "Not like animals. They do not wish to harm us. We were all brothers and sisters in arms. We must think about this. Rash action, like our friend suggests, would only lead to our downfall."

He flicked his cigarette away, and indicated to Ivy. "Ivy, you can lead as many of us as will follow you North, or even across the sea, to France, or Ireland. What will greet you there, I couldn't say. You can carry on our teachings. Find somewhere to re-establish our way. The rest of you, scatter. Carry on our goals; gather knowledge, protect it. Share it amongst yourselves. When the time is right, when Mother is gone, we can go back. Make things right. That's all."

Ivy nodded and sat down, speaking quietly with a larger woman sat next to her. The group began to talk amongst themselves, as Walker turned away. Charlie made his way over, carefully picking his way through the heavily armed walkers.

"Well, Walker. That was certainly somethin'. So that's it, you lot are splittin' up? Scatterin' to the four corners of the Earth, never to be heard from again?" He sipped at his drink, "Think that fella had a point, mind. You can't go runnin' away, tail between your legs forever." He laughed.

Walker turned to him, "Enough Charlie, we're not running. We're being careful."

Charlie nodded as he sipped again, "Fair enough, fair enough. You gonna be needing anything mate?"

Walker shook his head, and motioned to the boy.

"Ah," Charlie said, eyes flashing, "Your protégé. I've heard about you, son," He said to the boy, "The lad with no name."He chuckled nastily.

"Charlie. Enough. I'll speak to you later. Boy, come here."

Charlie winked again, and waved jovially at them as he left. The boy padded to Walker's side, glaring at the retreating figure of the bald little man.

"I don't like him. I can't read him properly."

Walker nodded. "He can be a bit showy, but that's his nature, for want of a better word. As to why you can't read him, well, it's important to remember that it's a person's *emotions* that make them readable, but never mind that for now. Boy, a question for you; what happened here?"

The boy thought, rubbing his chin. "The walkers challenged you. That woman, Ivy, started it, and Idris made it worse. But you turned it around. What did you say to him?"

Walker waved a hand as he rummaged in his satchel. "Unimportant, boy. What did you learn?"

"Learn? The boy asked, uncertainly.

"Yes," Walker replied slowly. "Learn. What did you take from this?"

The boy scratched his chin again. "Well. That the best way to deal with aggression, especially from those that should obey you, is to call them out. Make them smaller."

Walker glanced up at him, "Not entirely wrong, boy, but not quite right either. Remember our fight, in the farm? You attacked with all your strengths, and aggression, and still you failed. This was a similar occasion. Idris is... a good philosopher. Strong, quick, clever. But not clever enough."

He straightened up. "What I did was find his weakness. I didn't rise to his attack, but weakened it through my disregard of it. It's about adapting to the situation. If I had taken his offer for a fight, I'd have been beaten. Or worse." He shouldered his pack. "Do you understand?"

The boy hesitated, but nodded, "I think so. When you can't win by fighting, you win by being clever."

Walker nodded. "Now, boy, go to the bar. Here," he flicked a dull pound coin to him, "And buy us both a whiskey. I need a drink. But I have some matters to attend to first. Just remember the lessons from today. I'll see you in a moment."

He headed back down the room, towards the waiting walkers. Some of them rose to him immediately, clasping his gauntleted hand and talking in low voices.

The boy watched for a short while, and then headed into the bar, to await his master.

28

Walker stopped at the bottom of the stairs and lit his cigarette, cupping his hand against his face to shelter it from the wind. He inhaled and stretched, shifting the weight of his books across his shoulder. The machinery on his back whined and clunked, reminding him he needed to find an artificer at some point.

He wandered across the street and headed back the way they had come earlier; it was still busy out here even now, the city never truly slept. He stopped at a mobile vendor and bought some more tobacco, as well as some papers, and stowed them in a pocket. He grabbed a small, savoury pastry and chewed it as he walked.

He saw what he had been looking for, and chuckled to himself. He shook his head, finished the pastry, and took another drag of his cigarette.

The alley. Hopefully the reprobate was still in there.

Walker thumbed the safety on his pistol off, just in case, and made his way to the open mouth between the buildings. He peered cautiously around the corner of the alley, looking for signs of life. There was nothing. The man appeared to have gone. Walker slid fluidly into the alleyway, unholstering his revolver as he did so.

The sounds and glare of the city died behind him, leaving a dull bass rumble. Walker stepped quietly into the shadows, scanning for any sign of movement.

There was a sudden movement ahead, a flash of darker shadow in the gloom. Walker raised his pistol and darted forward, clutching at the shape.

The junkie hung in his grip, grinning. He had removed his helmet, and Walker could see pale grey eyes, deeply sunken into purplish sockets. His gaunt frame looked worse for the darkness of the alley and he was shaking.

Before Walker could speak, the creature chuckled dryly, pointing to his eyes. "Hindsight isn't as helpful as Insight, and half again as good as foresight."

Walker shook him roughly, he was like a doll in Walker's grip, "Stop babbling, wastrel. Charlie sent me."

The man giggled, staring at Walker unseeingly. "Old tin man sent you, but he's got no heart. The man from the tower is here. He will say to put away your gun, and you should."

Walker growled, "Why would I listen to you? You're unarmed. And even if you were, I could outshoot you."

The man tilted his head to one side, still smiling. "Maybe so, maybe so. But could you outshoot them?"

He pointed behind Walker, who turned. Several men stood at the mouth of the alley. Even in the gloom their helmets gleamed. Bookmen, Walker thought. Some had their rifles aimed up at him; he was out gunned. One of them called out to him.

"Put it away; rebel walkers aren't permitted to carry as it is."

Walker glanced back at the junkie. He lowered his pistol, slowly, and slid it back into its holster.

The little man wrenched free of Walker's grip and dropped clumsily to the ground, grinning at him. He turned to the soldiers. "I'll be back soon, and right as rain. Right?"

One of the soldiers was holding the helmet the junkie had been wearing when Walker last saw him. He raised it nonchalantly and threw it at the ground, where it shattered. The junkie's smile slowly sunk from his face, and his mouth twisted down, unpleasantly. His pale eyes stared mournfully at the destroyed eggshell pieces before him. The soldier laughed at his displeasure, and spat on the broken shards.

Before he could speak, a voice came from behind the soldiers. "I suggest you leave."

The men parted, and the tall, slim figure of the Librarian paced gently through. It was Michael, the head of the Order based in this area. He was dressed in his favoured black; black cape, the cracked, weathered leather flowed from his shoulders, like dark wings, limp before flight; black hat, wider and higher than Walker's; inky, black visor, shining darkly over that thin face which solemnly extended to a point below it.

Walker glared up at him. The Librarian looked impassively back.

"So," he intoned, "Here we are. Once again." He shook his head and walked past Walker, bending to look the junkie in the eye. "Time for you to leave. Don't make me say it again."

The small man ignored him, still staring at the fractured helmet. The Librarian prodded him, bringing the man back round. He looked up at Walker, focusing properly for the first time, peeled grape eyes lost and forlorn. He turned and shuffled off awkwardly through the rubbish in the alley, mumbling.

Walker continued to glower up at the Librarian. He was tall, taller than Walker, but slighter of build. His armour was new and well maintained, oily blackness giving an effect of dark efficiency next to Walker's scratched, dust scored, uncared for chest piece.

The Librarian straightened up and turned back to Walker. "So, you're still playing this game, then?" He looked Walker up and down, disapprovingly. "I notice you've changed your revolver. Lighter frame, looks newer. I wonder why."

He clucked like a hen, "And what are you today, I wonder? A mercenary? Private detective? Or are you still playing at being a walker?" He looked down at Walkers satchel, the rough shape of the books inside answering his question.

"Carpenter, take his satchel, please."

One of the Bookmen nodded and strode forward. As he reached for the strap of the bag, Walker gave a guttural bark and grabbed his wrist, twisting it up and forcing the man to his knees.

Instantly the other soldier's rifles were pointed at him, humming menacingly. Walker could hear the pleasant voice of the targeting systems in their helmets confirming his presence.

The Librarian sighed. "Please, let him go. No one needs to die here. Not this time."

Walker grunted and let the man go, who fell, grabbing his wrist. "What do you want?"

He sighed again and took off his hat, running a gloved hand through his salt and pepper hair. "I want you to stop this, as usual. Get up, Carpenter. He didn't even break it. "

Carpenter scrambled up, furious. "Fucking Walkers." He clenched a fist and drew it back, but the Librarian put a hand softly on his arm.

The bookman lowered his arm and turned away, muttering.

The Librarian continued, "We will be taking the satchel, Walker. You know the rules. No unlicensed distribution. No free walkers."

He held out a hand to Walker, who merely stared at it, mind racing. He was going to take the books.

"Come on, Walker. We haven't got all day. It's very late, in fact. Hand the books over, and I will consider you gone. I'm giving you a fair chance. *Another* one. Don't waste it. *Again.*"

Walker looked down at the ground. He numbly lifted the satchel strap over his head, feeling the weight of the books within. He was taking them, and there was nothing he could do. He handed them over to the Librarian, who took the pack carefully. Walker stalked past, pushing roughly through the soldiers and headed towards Charlie's bar.

The Librarian sighed again and watched him go. He shook his head and headed out of the alleyway, the soldiers falling in behind him.

29

13 years ago...

The market was busy; people bustled in and around stalls and shops as the sun beat down overhead. Walker had removed his cloak and rolled his sleeves up, enjoying the heat on his bare forearms. He had taken off his hat, too, which he carried. The boy was ahead, haggling with one of the stalls owner, trying to trade some tobacco for the honey they had found in an old, abandoned shop a while back.

Walker smiled as he watched the boy at work. He smiled and laughed, setting the merchant at ease with the right body language, the right kind of speech, mimicking the midlands accent perfectly. He certainly knew how to read people now; it seemed natural to him. Walker felt a certain pride; the boy had come such a long way. He rubbed his chin thoughtfully, as the boy loped back to him.

"Managed to get this," he offered the wraps of tobacco, but Walker waved him away.

"Keep them, you earned it."

The boy raised an eyebrow quizzically, but pocketed one of the wraps, handing the remaining two to Walker. "For you."

Walker smiled and took the tobacco. "Thanks, boy. What else did we need?"

The boy rolled himself a cigarette, pulling apart a clump and thumbing it smooth like Walker had shown him.

Without looking up, he replied, "We need to go to the artificers, repair the joints on your back lifting plate," he glanced up, smirking, "Can't have you falling apart on me Old Man, I might need you to carry something important."

Walker laughed as the boy lit his cigarette. "This is true." He began to roll himself a cigarette. "Anything else?"

The boy exhaled, looking up at the sun, squinting in its glare. He rubbed at the soft stubble growing at his chin, before turning to Walker. We could do with some food, the bread's gone old. And my boots are running thin on the soles."

Walker lit his own cigarette, nodding. "All good, but I think there's one place we should go first. This way."

Walker turned from the main street and headed towards the mouth of the shaded alley that marked the beginning of the tools district.

"Walker, what do we need down here?"

Walker smiled to himself. "Just follow, lad, you'll see soon enough."

The sounds and smells of metal work greeted their nostrils; hot coals, steaming water baths, sweating beats, oxen and mules moving loads, or powering mills. Bright sparks flashed orange and yellow from the shadows of the shops lining the alley, men and women shouted to one another; masters scolded apprentices and customers haggled over prices.

Walker glanced back at the boy, and noted with pleasure his vetted interest; he was examining every stall, talking to the craftspeople, asking and learning. Walker allowed this; they were in no real rush, not today. He ambled easily down the widening street, looking.

There, he thought. Towards the end of the street, where the road turned right and led back to the main road, was the shop.

A rusted gun hung from the wall above the door, a revolver, similar to Walker's. He nodded and turned to find the boy, who was bent examining a man who seemed to be building a large cylinder, tubes and piping covered its surface

"Here, lad; come now, let's go."

The boy looked up, patted the worker on the shoulder, and jogged over to Walker. "They were building a new fuel system, it melts plastics and rubbish down into petrol, really clever stuff, they said that—"

Walker waved him quiet, "I'm sure, lad, I'm sure. But this is better."

He put his hand amiably on the boy's shoulder and gestured up at the shop.

"It's... a gunsmith?" the boy asked.

Walker nodded, giving him a friendly pat, "Indeed it is, my lad. It's time for you to have your own."

He led the way into the smoky interior, the heat blasting out as he opened the door. They entered into a wide, high ceilinged room, cluttered with tools. The floor immediately ahead was occupied by a counter, almost as long as the room was wide, but only a couple of feet wide.

The counter, and almost every wall of the room, was covered with parts; springs, catches, firing pins, hammers; it seemed as though every part from every gun was somewhere in the shop. There were no bare walls, although there was a furnace, its hood covered with ornate carvings, intricate details lit by the glow from the fires below.

From somewhere in the shop the faint strains of violins and other strings could be heard, barely audible over the hungry grumble of the furnace. Walker smiled, she hadn't lost her keen tastes, then.

The boy's eyes widened, trying to take everything in at once; he moved about the store as if in a trance, touching things, picking up parts and examining them. He probably could've continued forever if not for the stern tone from the back of the shop.

"I hope you aren't thinking of taking that, young man?"

The boy started and dropped the part he was looking at; it hit the floor and came apart with the merry tinkling that can be heard when a lot of hard work is undone. He immediately dropped to the floor, attempting to pick up and reassemble what he had dropped, but Walker touched his arm.

"Stand up boy, we can sort that later. Meet Sasha."

He waved an arm to where the voice had come from, indicating the woman standing there. She hadn't changed at all, Walker thought to himself. Originally an instructor with the Order, she was one of the few who had left peacefully during Father's reign, choosing a life of practical knowledge; her ability to fashion and maintain weapons was second to none.

She descended the stairs leading down into the shop, radiating stern serenity. She was dark and ghostlike in the gloom of the shop, her face angular in the sullen glow from the furnace, her square shoulders lit from behind. The music was louder now that the back door was open.

"Walker," she nodded to him.

Walker nodded his response, speaking solemnly. "This young man is in need of a weapon suitable of his skills."

"This is the boy that was at the meeting?"

Walker nodded.

"He has not grown much," she looked critically at the boy, who was still holding one of the pieces he had dropped, "And does this one not have a name? This... boy?"

Walker felt a familiar pang of regret as he looked at the boy.

Sasha pressed on, her sharp accent picking her words out, "Well? Or shall I call you the boy with no name?"

The boy's face glowed red in the light, his embarrassment hidden by the embers in the furnace. "Just boy, I think."

Walker watched Sasha, who shrugged. She came around the long counter, and they could see her properly. Her hair had gone grey, Walker noticed, and she kept it tied up in a bun atop her head.

She was wearing leathers, loose fitting, to protect her from stray embers and blasting heat. Her furnace goggles hung from her neck, and her hands were heavily gauntleted, and embers were smudged across her face, darker motes of black against the ebony of her skin.

She stopped in front of the boy and eyed him up. He smiled as the boy tried to straighten up; Sasha was still easily a head taller than even Walker.

"This one is of age, Walker?" she peered over at him, "Surely not?"

The boy's chest swelled and he spoke for himself. "I'm seventeen."

Sasha looked sternly down at him. "And this means that you are old enough?"

The boys face hardened as he frowned slightly. "It does."

Sasha folded her arms. "Well," she said, "He is certainly confident enough, for a boy with no name. On your head be it, Walker." She headed back to her side of the counter and pulled up a low stool, indicating that they should do the same.

Walker seated himself, his fractured armour squealing protest.

Sasha's face screwed up, as if in pain, "*Mój Boże,* Walker! You know the sound of machinery being... tortured makes a mockery of what I do. There is an armourer three shops down. Selly is a good man."

Walker nodded agreement. Sasha took a deep breath, eyes closed, apparently concentrating on the music behind her. Her eyes slowly opened, and she continued. "Now, boy, I will ask questions, and you will answer." She threw a sharp look at Walker, "Truthfully. I know your friend's reputation for... bending the truth. Mark my words and be honest, if you lie, you will not receive the correct weapon, and will never master it. Understand?"

The boy nodded, looking nervous but less red than he had before.

"Which is more important, speed and agility, or brute strength and power?"

The boy answered immediately, "It depends on the situation. A hare is faster than a dog, but the dog is stronger than the hare. But, a man could outthink them, and beat them both."

Sasha's face remained impassive as she continued. "If one has the ability to act in a given situation, should they always do so? Are they obliged to act, regardless of their personal motives?"

Again, the boy's answer was fast. "If the action worsens a situation, then inaction is always preferable."

Sasha tilted her head slightly, "I will give you an example. There is a man drowning in a river, the current of which is powerful and strong, and surely able to drown the strongest swimmer. It is thought that he is a thief, and may also be a murderer. But," she held up a leather clad finger, "You cannot know until he is rescued whether he is guilty or not. Do you risk your life to save a potentially innocent man, or allow that this man is consigned to his fate."

The boy looked back, thinking. "It depends on the situation, again. Are there others there to help me? If so, what tools and equipment do we have? And who claimed him to be a thief? The question has too many variables. I don't think there is an answer."

Walker held back a smile as Sasha frowned.

"That is an answer in itself, boy," she replied. "Final question, boy: do those with the power to act have the right to do so?"

The boy raised his eyebrow. "I... don't think I understand."

Sasha clucked and leaned in. "Come, boy, you were doing well. I will rephrase it, more *specifically*, just for you. If one has the power to take life, do they also have the right?"

The boy glanced over at Walker. "I..."

Sasha interjected, before Walker could speak. "You must answer. Not him."

Walker remained passive, and the boy looked away. "It depends on... If they...," He cleared his throat and looked the woman in the face. "Yes."

Sasha nodded, seemingly satisfied with these answers. "You take after your master, boy. Speed and power matter equally to men who not only act, but think, and not only think, but think accordingly."

She rose from her stool and headed towards the back wall, where a series of drawers were padlocked into the wall. Selecting a key from the chain at her waist, she unlocked one of these drawers and retrieved the weapon.

As she brought it to the table, the furnace shone darkly from its oiled surface; a pistol, lighter and newer than Walker's own, with a revolving chamber. Walker saw how the boy watched it, calmly, almost serenely, noting the hunger in his eyes. Sasha beckoned to him, "Come around, boy" she commanded.

The boy did as he was told, joining her on the opposite side of the table. The shadows rose about him, darkening his face. Walker could see the fiery orange glow reflected from the gun shining in the boy's eyes.

"Take it; hold it and feel the weight."

He did so, lifting the gun reverently, pointing and sighting along the length of the room.

"How is it?" The smith answered.

The boy continued to look down the sight. "It feels... good."

Sasha shook her head, plucking the gun from his grasp. "Tools are not good, nor bad. They perform a task. They do a job. The owner is 'good' or 'bad'. Never the tool. You understand, or has this man failed to teach you anything?" She scoffed, "Good and bad. Pfft."

91

The boy frowned down at Sasha, but Walker intervened. "He knows, Smith. He is learning, and learning well."

Sasha eyed Walker's visor for some time, before shrugging. "*Niech tak będzie.* 'Tis not the place of some lowly master gunsmith to tell *the* Walker himself what is, and what should be."

She gave the gun back to the boy, and leaned under the table to fetch a holster, which she also handed over.

"What do you say, boy?" asked Walker.

The boy attached the holster at his waist, and slid the gun into it. "My thanks, ma'am."

Sasha waved a gauntleted hand at him dismissively. "I do not want your thanks boy. Walker, what do you have for me this time?"

Walker stood, tucking the stool back into its place under the table. He reached into his satchel and drew out the gifts; a book on fine arts and a disc, usable in some old world tech items. This one played music when inserted into the device Sasha was listening to now..

Sasha smiled as she took them from him, the first time she had done so since they had arrived, and examined the book. "You never cease to surprise me, Walker. My thanks."

Walker nodded, closing the clasps on his satchel. "Come, boy. Time we left."

The boy nodded and made his way from the shop, hand resting on the weapon slung at his hip. As Walker went to follow, Sasha called to him.

"Walker, one more thing. *He* was here, looking for you. He's not happy. Idris has already paid the price. Be careful."

Walker turned from the doorway and looked at Sasha. "I heard, Smith. Idris was a good walker."

Sasha shook her head. "It's a fool's errand you find yourself on, Richard."

Despite her cold outwards appearance, he knew she hid a softer side; her first love was of fine arts, music, and history. Her skill with metals and tools was unmatched by any man he had ever met. The dying embers of the furnace cast shadows over her face, blacking out her eyes, causing her hair to shine a dim crimson.

Walker nodded and left the shop, stepping into the sunlight of the outside world.

30

Daisy was bored. She had gone through drunkenness and was now worryingly sober again. The bar was quiet now, everyone had been sent home, or at least thrown out, and only Charlie and herself remained, aside from a few bar staff cleaning the bar and sweeping.

He sat opposite her in the dark, quietly smoking on a cigar. They had been playing cards, and talking. He still made her uneasy, but he had been pleasant enough.

Daisy picked dully at the chicken and chips she hadn't finished earlier, as Charlie poured himself another drink from the bottle on their table. "So, Daisy, why're you following him? The walker, I mean. What are you after?"

He offered her the bottle, which she took, pouring herself another shot.

"I...," she paused, looking at Charlie. He had taken his shades off. She watched him and sipped her drink, "He promised me something, when I was younger," she hesitated, "I thought he could help change things."

He nodded and took a puff on his cigar. "Let me guess, he found you as a kid? Showed you a book?"

She eyed him quizzically.

He shrugged, "Before you ask, educated guess."

She took another scrap of chicken, "I don't know why we're here though. He doesn't tell me anything.""

"The man is certainly a closed book," Charlie laughed softly and finished his drink, "He'd like that, don't you think. Being likened to a book."

Daisy swallowed and took another sip, "Why do you think we're here, Charlie?"

"Well, I deal in things, little lady. Most of those things a man like Walker ain't interested in, know what I mean? But I do dabble," here he leaned in conspiratorially, "In tools of higher education, and particular learning."

"Books, then?"

"Bingo, right in one. But keep it hush-hush, yeah?" He laughed again, obviously finding himself to be too funny. Daisy rolled her eyes and poked at the chicken carcass in front of her.

"Walker collects any books he finds, Charlie. What would make him come here, to you, today?"

He tilted his head like a dog, "I dunno my love. Could be anything. Like I said, man's a closed book." He poured from the bottle again, and asked her, "Why is it you think you're *here*, Daisy? Not in my club, specifically; what is it you think you're doing out here, away from home, all alone?"

She shook her head. "I suppose I'm learning." She plucked at the chicken again, "You know, how to become a proper walker, with the Order. All that."

Charlie laughed again, throwing his head back, "A walker with the Order!" He hooted, "That's great!"

Daisy scowled at him as he dabbed at his eyes, "What's so funny?"

The laughter trailed off, and Charlie looked at her. "Wait, you're bein' serious? Blimey."

When she continued to glower, he shook his head.

"He's draggin' you 'round all over and you don't even know why? Thought he'd have learned the first time." He got up and walked over to the bar, reached over and grabbed another two bottles, which he uncorked and brought back to the table.

"You might need one of these, got a fair bit to cover."

She reluctantly accepted one of the bottles as Charlie resumed his seat, shifting until he was comfortable. He poured himself a snifter and sipped it. "I won't start from the very beginnin' or we'll be 'ere all bleedin' night. So we'll start post crisis. You know what the crisis was, right?"

Daisy shrugged, "I never got taught properly. I know something happened a long time ago, and most of the people, people who could afford to anyway, left. My Mum says they went to the skies, but that sounds stupid."

Charlie poured from the fresh bottle, smoky whiskey splashed into his glass. He swirled it, sniffed, and sipped, before pouring into Daisy's glass. "Not so stupid, actually. Yeah, people moved off, round about 2195, to colonise the moons of Jupiter, or something daft like that. I know they went to Mars, at any rate."

Daisy opened her mouth to question this, but Charlie waved her quiet.

"Anyways, all we need to know is that something big, real big, happened, and changed how things worked. Governments came and went, lotsa fightin' happened; long story short, we were left with the world as you see it now." He looked away for a second, then added, "Or rather, the country as you see it now. Doubt you've ever left England."

She shook her head, and he shrugged listlessly.

"So there was this group, yeah, called the People's Reclamation Republic. They were all for people rising back up, taking what had been left by the leaders what had abandoned them; fixing technology, collecting knowledge and all that jazz. They started the Philosophers, the ones you know about. But they were pretty pants at first. They tried to gather things up; books, papers, computers – you won't know what a computer is, of course; like a super book, one that could do anything – and they tried to do it by force. Which people didn't like. They fought back, and killed the Philosophers, the first ones, who were just scholars really. Not soldiers, no good at fighting."

Daisy sat back, stunned. "How do you know all this?"

Charlie waved her quiet, "Hush, got a lot to cover." He drummed his thick fingers on his chin thoughtfully.

"Where was I... oh yeah, so; the Republic decided they needed some 'arder blokes to gather up all this valuable stuff, and keep it safe, so they made a new order. The second cohort. They even made an academy for 'em, to train 'em up, using ex-soldiers and that, proper like. Took kiddies, young as tots, and started fresh. These blokes grew up with the Order, became tough, and smart. They valued their work more than they valued the people they were workin' on, and things got messy.

"Now, maybe 'bout ten years later, the third lot of Philosophers was trained. These guys were even tougher, and they had technology on their side, amour like what your pal Walker wears and whatnot. The government found this old stash of pre-crisis weapons, see, and thought of no better way of proving their principles about 'knowledge' than equipping the guys they employed with some of it."

He paused to steal a chip from Daisy's plate. He chewed it, making appreciative noises, before continuing.

"Nothin' tastier than a stolen chip, eh?" He winked, and cleared his throat. "Now, these philosophers, they were still taught that the people who were harbouring their books and so on were bad, and below them. So there was this incident, nasty one, where a whole village got killed over some dispute. Out east ways, I think." He looked at his drink, swirling it slightly, "Or was it up north?

"Anyway, people obviously had had enough about this time, and they started to make themselves heard. Lots of fighting between the Order and the regular folk. Bloody, and 'orrible.

"'Bout this time, a geeze took control of the Republic. People called him the Father, 'cos he was one of the oldest guys in the republic; started the training program, effectively bore the Order, straight from his own loins."

He chuckled at his own joke, "Now, this Father, he starts to go a bit bonkers, with the power and that. Gets all paranoid, tells the order that they had enough books, and knowledge and technology, and decides that the public don't deserve their services; he wants to keep all the knowledge and the power for the Order.

"Enter Mother. God knows why she got called that. Maybe it was 'cause her and Father argued all the time, sort of in-joke maybe. This girl, she's got a hot head, and the skills to match, and says that Father has lost his way. But she bides her time, following orders, tryin' to do good from the inside.

Daisy spoke, "Mother was a walker then?"

Charlie shrugged, sipping his drink. "Not exactly. Born of two philosophers, probably on a moonless night, or summink soppy like that."

"Anyway," he continued, "This went on for a few years, things getting' worse and worse between Father and Mother. Then one day, BOOM," He slammed the table dramatically, making Daisy jump, "Someone offed Father, killed 'im. Mother took over, tried to take the Order back to what they was all about in the first place; protecting books, saving knowledge, getting ready to share it out again, amongst the people, for the people."

Daisy interrupted again, "Wait, wait, wait. The Order is not 'for the people'. They go around stealing books, ruining lives. That's what the Walkers are for. They fight the Order, share books around."

Charlie raised an eyebrow, "Is that so? How many of his books is ole Walker lettin' you carry then?"

Daisy paused, thinking. Walker had never let her even hold the book satchel, let alone touch one of his books.

"Hang on," she exclaimed, "He gave me this!"

She got out her copy of *Treasure Island*, and held it out for Charlie to look. He took it from her, flicking through the first few pages.

"Sorry, love." He read, and clucked, "This ain't even a third edition. And it's a story. Stories aren't worth that much. The man loves 'real' knowledge. Books on machines, guns, thinking. All that malarkey. He's a genius when it comes to machines, come to think of it."

He offered her the book back, which she took, feeling disheartened. Walker had given her a book he hadn't even cared for.

"Where were we?" Charlie tapped his forehead dramatically. "Ah, got it. So yeah, Mother's in charge now, right? She's getting' things back on track, undoin' the damage old Father did, makin' the Order about knowledge again, not power. That's where your man Walker comes in. Seems that he disagreed with Mother, cheeky little sod. He was a teenager at the time though, and you know what they get like."

He flashed his irritating wink again. "So, Walker decides he knows better than Mother, and challenges her for power over the Order, but she refuses. Good thing too; she taught him, so he woulda stood a snowball's chance in a bloody hot place, if you ask me. So, bein' a stroppy teenager and that, Walker leaves, takin' a few of his mates with him, some of his 'cohort', as they like to say, along with some of the older lads and ladies from the Order. Since then, they've been fartin' about, doin' as they please. Think that about covers it, love."

Daisy's thoughts raced. "So wait, walkers aren't a part of the Order?"

Charlie shook his head, "Not strictly. They were. Damn fine members, from what they've all told me. But no," he swirled his drink, "Not *strictly* a part in any 'official' capacity." He waggled his fingers. "Any questions?"

Daisy scratched her head, "Too many, Charlie. What are the Walkers, then?"

Charlie grinned at her, "Well, it's in the name, innit? Walker, walkers. That's why they call themselves that, apparently. You coulda worked it out. Maybe that's what he's been waitin' for."

Daisy shook her head, confused, "I was never sure."

Charlie shrugged, "Never mind Daisy, me old china. Now you know. And knowin' is half the battle, and all that good stuff."

Daisy sat staring. What did she know? Had walker lied to her? Well, she thought, he hadn't technically; he hadn't actually *told* her anything. "How do you know all this Charlie?"

"Well, I was there through it all, weren't I? Seen it all, even the crisis. Good times, good times." He leant back in the booth, sipping at his drink.

"Saw? Wait, if you saw it all, that makes you... hundreds of years old! How?"

He waved her quiet again. "I don't like talkin' about that, love. All you need to remember is Father started things goin' downhill, Mother rose up and whacked him, and Walker went off in a hissy fit."

Daisy looked down into her glass, then up at Charlie. He was looking towards the door.

There was a loud crash. A bouncer burst through the main door, horizontally, landing spread-eagled on the ground. Walker stepped over to him and stormed over to the table.

"Walker, mate, what'cha wack Rob f—"

Daisy watched, shocked, as he grabbed Charlie by the throat, hoisting him easily into the air.

Charlie gasped, trying to speak. "Walker, what..."

Walker growled and squeezed harder. Daisy watched as Charlie struggled feebly as something whirred, high pitched and frantic.

"Walker!" She cried, jumping to her feet. "What's going on?"

He ignored her and maintained his vice-like grip. She had to do something.

She brought her arm down on Walker's, loosening his hold on Charlie. She pushed the little man out of the way, as Walker whirled on her.

"What are you doing, girl?"

He towered over her, fists clenched. She had never seen him this angry.

"What are *you* doing?" She shouted back. She squared up to him, blocking him from Charlie. They glared at each other for what felt like an eternity, before Daisy spoke.

"Enough of this. You wanna know about your books? So what? They clearly mean fuck all to you." She grabbed *Treasure Island* from the table and brandished it at Walker. "This book? The reason I left, got myself mixed up in this shit? You never gave a damn, did you?"

She threw the book. It struck Walker in the chest. He flinched slightly, but didn't catch it. "Give me a reason not to leave right now."

Walker looked from her to Charlie, "What did you tell her?"

Before Charlie could answer, Daisy spoke, "No, Walker, talk to me. He only told me what you should have told me the day I went with you. You're not actually a part of the Order, are you? You're part of that other group. I guess it was as obvious as Charlie said."

She narrowed her eyes at him, and continued, "So you have to promise me something Walker, if you want me to come with you."

Walker looked at her, lips set in a thin line, "Why would I want you to come with me?"

She thought, quickly, decided to play her ace. "I know about you, now. That could be dangerous."

Walker stood, quietly. Daisy watched, tensed. Finally, Walker sighed.

"Fair enough. Let me settle with Charlie, girl. We'll talk after."

She frowned at him, but bit her tongue. Walker leant on the table, bringing himself closer to Charlie, who had sat and begun rubbing his neck. "My books, Charlie."

"You prick, you've gone and duffed up me hydraulics, gonna cost me a pretty penny."

Daisy raised her eyebrow at this, but allowed Walker to talk.

"They took my books." Walker's words came out heavy, and slow

"I... don't know what you're talking about. That job was genuine—" Walker slapped him, hard. Charlie's face turned, and Daisy could hear a curious ringing noise. He piped up indignantly. "You're lucky I rolled with that, big man, or you'd be nursin' a couple o' broken fingers."s

Walker ignored him, jerking him upwards again, so they were eye to visor. "You set me up. They took my books. You better know something, or I will kill you."

He dropped Charlie, who steadied himself and made a show of brushing off his suit. "*Kill me?* Hilarious," he snorted, rearranging his lapels. "And by *they* I assume you mean the Bookies? You musta been followed, mate. Nuffin' to do with me. And that's a computational certainty, you can trust me on that."

He tried to wink at Daisy, but something from within him whirred. He rubbed at his throat again, glaring at Walker and opening his mouth to speak.

98

Walker slammed his hand onto the table before he could utter a word, "Enough damn it! Where are my books? How did they know I was here?"

Charlie glared at his hand and shook his head. "Bugger me, Walker, look at you mate! You come in to the city, dressed like that, with a bloody great bag o' what are clearly bloody great books in your bag. You saunter in 'ere, big as day, meet with me, and you know they watch me, and you expect no one to notice? Arrogant twat."

He picked up his glass and rubbed his throat again. "Won't be able to drink again till I get this sorted." He sighed and put the drink down.

"You don't need to drink, Charlie. Don't give me that."

Charlie glared at him, his eyes still flashing. "I know I don't *need* to drink, you arsehole. I like the taste."

He shook his head and sat down, wearily rubbing a hand over his shiny face, "Look, I said the men in black drink here, din't I? Stands to reason they 'eard us and followed you. It was what I was checking the girl for in the first place. Good job she stayed and all," he jerked a thumb towards Daisy, "They'd've killed her on sight."

Walker glared at him, but Daisy spoke first. "Why would they have killed me, and not him?"

Charlie looked glumly down at his drink, massaging where Walker had gripped him. "'Cos he knows the main man. Best fuckin' mates ain't they."

31

11 years ago...

Walker stretched as he took his seat at the bar. The lad was off scouring the small market nearby, and would be back shortly. For now, he had whiskey as his sole companion, which was fine.

The lad was nearing the end of what Walker could teach him, making them almost equals, but Walker saw no reason they couldn't continue to travel together; he had grown to enjoy the company. Sure, the boy still had some way to go, he thought as he quietly sipped at his whiskey, but who knew everything at his age? Michael, possibly, he mused, grinning and rubbing at the rough bristles on his chin.

99

The lad was fully grown, cheeky, arrogant and devious, but charming, with the intellect to match. Walker smiled to himself. Almost like looking into a mirror.

He was about to finish his drink, when someone sat next to him. "The man himself," Walker murmured.

Michael smiled softly and held up a finger, signalling for a whiskey. "Do you...?"

Walker shrugged and drank the last of his whiskey, "If you're buying."

Michael nodded and held up a second finger. The bartender retrieved a bottle and began to pour two glasses. "Leave the bottle," the waiter nodded, and Michael continued, "So, Richard."

Walker smiled to himself. "Call me Dick, Michael. You're the only one allowed, may as well make the most of it."

Michael frowned , eyes hidden behind his dark visor. "What are you doing around here," he paused on the unsavoury nickname, "Dick?"

Walker sipped the fresh glass the waiter had left, and looked at Michael, his eyes also hidden beneath his own silvery visor. "Just travelling through, chum," Michael flinched at the informality, "Just travelling through."

Michael sipped his own drink, slender fingers gripping the glass from below. "What is it you do these days, Richard?"

Walker shrugged. "This and that. Whatever I can. I get by." He sipped again. "Don't worry; I'm not considering becoming a mercenary, or a private eye, or anything like that."

The two men chuckled briefly, and sunk back to uncomfortable silence. Michael downed his whiskey and turned to Walker slightly.

"I know you have books, Richard. I know the Walkers are still operating."

Walker paused, thinking. Of course Michael knew, he always knew. "Nothing gets past you, eh Mike?"

Michael ignored the nickname. "Indeed. In fact, they made me Servile Philosopher for it."

Walker scowled briefly. How had he missed that? Out loud, he said, "Well done. So I assume you're here to arrest me, part of your duties?"

Michael smiled sadly and shook his head. "No, Richard, that was five years ago. I'm not the Servile Philosopher anymore."

Walker eyed him up warily.

Michael continued, "I'm the Librarian now."

Walker coughed up the whiskey he'd been drinking, spraying it on to the bar. There were some murmurs of wasting good booze, but they stopped as Michael turned sharply. He gazed coolly at the mutterers, before turning back to Walker.

"I know what you've been doing. Unlawfully withholding books, slowing the process down. And training that boy, teaching him our ways."

Walker stopped coughing and looked at Michael. His friend had always been slight, and too pale, but his new black cloak rendered him paler still, and made his cheeks look gaunt; his face appeared as though chiselled from blunt rock.

"I will let you go. Find somewhere safe to leave the books. There's an abandoned farmhouse up the road. We won't have to hurt anyone that way."

Walker swirled his whiskey slightly, "And the boy?"

Michael sighed and sipped again at his drink. "If there were a way for him to forget what you have taught him..." he finished his whiskey.

Walker stared down into his glass.

Michael nodded once. "I'm afraid it's the only way, Richard. Do all that I have said and we *will* leave you alone, I promise you. But fail, that is, keep the books and the boy, and I cannot help you." He pointed to Walker, "Get rid of the boy, let him go and teach him no more. Hopefully he will become a mercenary, and forget any... foolishness you have put in his head."

He lowered his hand. "Goodbye Richard. Hopefully we never see each other again."

He stood up and flicked some coins onto the counter, leaving Walker at the bar. He strode outside, people moving aside as he went.

Walker watched him go and turned back to his glass. He sighed and drained his drink, refilling it with the bottle Michael had left behind.

He sat alone, pondering gloomily, rubbing at his chin as the bar chattered inconsequentially around him, oblivious to the darkness behind his visor.

32

Daisy kept her arms folded, staring at Walker. "Something you need to tell me?

Walker turned slightly to her, rubbed his chin, and gave a half shrug. Daisy moved a hand in an impatient twirling gesture.

101

He grunted, gave a final raspy scratch of his stubble, and spoke, "He means Michael. The Librarian. An old," he hesitated slightly, and his left hand spasmed into a fist. He exhaled slightly, "an old friend of mine. He was waiting for me. Took my books."

She nodded, and he turned to Charlie, who was still fiddling with his rumpled suit. "The junkie. He was working with them."

Charlie shrugged, and his shoulder clicked as it went up and down. "Well, like you said, he's a junkie; works for any old someone who pays him." He clicked again and something whirred inside him, "Blimey Walker, you've really ballsed me up 'ere."

He reached up to his neck and pressed a gentle finger at a previously seamless patch of skin, which retracted to reveal wires, cables and blinking lights.

Daisy, bemused despite herself, spoke up, "So you are a robot. Only heard about them once, back home."

He bristled slightly, poking around inside the newly opened gap, "I ain't a *robot,* girl. That means slave. I'm an android."

Walker now folded his arms, "Charlie?"

The grey man grunted and continued to fiddle, "Yeah, yeah. Look, you know what addicts are like, right? Don't matter what they're in to, they'll do what they can to get their fix. Probably offered him some new VR gear, or something... bugger!"

He swore as he pushed something into place with a crunch. His eyes flashed once before returning to their previous twinkle.

"That's better. For now, at least. You'll be fixin' this proper before you leave, mind you."

Walker continued to glare at him. "After. First, tell me what happened. They took my books."

Charlie pressed at his neck again and the flap of skin reattached itself; it was impossible to see there had been a sizable opening a second before. He turned to Walker, scowling. "Boo-bloody-hoo Mister Walker, what a shame. Like they were your books anyway."

Daisy watched as Walker leant in, closer to Charlie, bending low over the table. He was seething, his teeth gritted angrily, spitting every word like lead shot. "Charlie. I want my books back."

Charlie leaned away slightly; Daisy wondered idly if androids could smell too.

"Look, calm down Walker. The books weren't my fault, okay? If I could help get 'em back, I would. But he'll be takin' them to the library, for processin' and that. They're gone" He picked up his drink, then remembered himself. He grumbled and put the glass back down.

102

"Seems to me, if those books was so important, you wouldn't have risked 'em coming to see ole Charlie for something more specific, would you?"

Daisy turned to Walker, "He's got a point, Walker. I want to know what we're doing here, too."

Walker turned to her, lips stern, "What is it you want to know?"

She gazed levelly back, seeing herself reflected by the dull lights in his visor. When she didn't respond, he shook his head.

"I don't need to tell you anything. You can leave whenever you want."

Daisy stared at him, mouth open slightly, "Leave? Leave to where? I can't go home, I have nowhere to go, no one to *bother* going home for! You've brought me here, *asked* me to come here, remember?" She stooped and grabbed *Treasure Island*, which she brandished like a sword. "You made a promise to me, all those years ago. I kept my end of things, and I've lost too much for it. So tell me; what are we doing here?"

He looked down at the book; she could see the muscles in his face working silently, tensing and rippling like bunched snakes. Finally, he replied, with a sigh.

"Okay, girl. I'll tell you. We're here to see Charlie for a special book. The *officium historia*."

He sat down, pulling the whiskey bottle to him. He took a long swig as she stood mouthing what he had said.

"The what?"

Walker glanced at her, but Charlie answered, "The Service Records, doll. Only reason he'd want that is if he were teachin' a class on how to send people to sleep the quickest. What are you, Walker, daft? No one can get that book."

Daisy also sat, and she pushed her glass over to Walker. He looked down at it, then filled it. He took another swig from the bottle and exhaled slowly, turning back to Charlie.

"Can you help me?"

Charlie rubbed absently at his neck again, "Buggered if I don't need that drink now, Walker."

Walker began to roll himself a smoke, "Charlie?"

"You'd have to get into the Library, you daft twat." He looked up at Walker, who gazed steadily back.

"Blimey. You're serious."

Charlie sat alone in the bar, sipping at his drink. Walker had patched up his neck well enough for now, reconnecting the hydraulic cable that was damaged when he had crushed his throat. The boy certainly knew his stuff, Charlie conceded.

Walker. The man had always been angry, but hell... He seemed worse these days, different, odd. Just... worse.

Poor girl, he mused, swirling the remains of his whiskey. Although, he allowed, she did seem to have a good grasp on things. Could be a match even for the 'mighty' Walker. He scoffed to himself in the silence of his club. Could be what he needs to sort him out, he reasoned.

He sipped at his drink again. Charlie had sent them to a contact of his, worked in 'repurposing items of value from one client to another', who knew some of the best ways up, in, around, under and over the city, and promised he could help them out.

The Library was old, part of the old university that had once sat so proudly at the top of the hill at the city centre, full of narrow passages, underground entryways, and other, more hidden secrets. Charlie was sure the Librarian knew every bloody 'secret' way into his sanctuary but hey.

He stood and made his way to the bar, which he leant on, drink in hand. The cleaners had finished up and gone home, and the door had been fixed.

He reached into the cubby hole behind the liquor cabinet and retrieved his book.

Charlie knew the title well, despite the lack of any covers and the first twenty pages. He settled to read, and think, and drink, two relics left in the remains of the old world.

Benny 'No Names' Harrison scurried along the walkway, rain pattering down around him in the morning darkness, drowning out his footfalls. It was more than he could say for the big man crouched behind him, whose lifter boots and rig were clinking and spitting every time the oaf clumped along the metal surface. The girl wasn't much better, splashing willy-nilly in all the puddles she didn't notice, and most of the puddles she did.

Charlie had offered Benny a lucrative deal if he could get the two fools as close to the Library as he could, but he was starting to have second thoughts. There had been more activity since last night, and the guards were more alert, patrolling the rooftop as well as the underground.

He looked behind him again, eyeing up his companions. The man was clearly a walker, illegal as they came. Heavy revolver slung at his hip, wide hat, old model T-400 visor hooked round his head, even older Pangolin plate armour, and a sour smell Benny could pick up even in the winds up here.

The girl was young, also wearing a visor, the model number eluded him for now, with an impractical half coat, leather, and blue jeans.

He sighed inwardly. Benny thought it'd be sensible to wear dark clothes, such as the dyed leather jacket and patched combats he had on currently.

"Amateurs." He muttered.

The big man turned his head up, into the rain, "Say something?"

Benny spat over the edge, and half turned. "Nothing, Walker. Just keep up."

They reached the end of the slippery metal walkway, and paused for breath behind a buttress. Benny flicked out his stick cam and poked it gently over the top, and out towards the library.

Through the screen on the base of the pole, he could make out the library, nestled among the skyscrapers of the city centre. Hover drones swirled and danced above the blue pulse emanating from the dome of the library itself. Metal gantries and cranes dotted about, making a perimeter around the vast concrete structure of the library proper.

The walker spoke, "So, thief, is there a way in?"

Benny ignored him, still scanning the scene before him. The foot traffic on the ground was minimal but, and here he zoomed the camera in as far as it would go, he could make out guards patrolling the gantries. He cursed softly and collapsed the camera.

"Well, bad news. The easy way in, which by no means was going to be easy, is now impossible."

The walker stayed passive, water pouring from his hat and down his cloak. The girl spoke in his place.

"Charlie mentioned underground walkways. Could we go that way?"

Benny grimaced. It wasn't that he was claustrophobic, he just had an aversion to walking underground through the filth of the city.

He sighed, "I'll bet he's loving the idea of sending us down there. It's true, there are old cellars, basements and tunnels dotted all over the city, from before the crisis. But I'll be damned if they don't stink to high heaven."

The walker scowled and leaned in closer. Benny, in turn, leaned slightly back. "Damn your personal hygiene, thief. Let's go."

Benny glared back at the man, "There will be guards, walker," he spat the word, "So be prepared. Come on, then. I hope you don't mind heights."

He grinned darkly at the two of them, motioned that they should move behind him, and slipped lightly under the railing and over the edge to his left, which opened out to the city.

35

Daisy watched with astonishment as their guide disappeared into the night. "Umm... where did he go?"

Walker wiped some rain from his visor and turned to her, "Looks like he jumped," he said, matter-of-factly.

Daisy looked from him, to where Benny had disappeared into the darkness, when she heard a cry from below.

"Are you coming? I'm not getting any dryer down here."

She summoned the courage to detach herself from the solid bricks and managed to peer over the edge of the metal walkway, sticking her head under the railing. Benny stood unharmed below them, arms akimbo like an angry mother.

Walker peered cautiously over the edge next to her, holding the rail to steady himself, "He's mad."

Benny called up to them again, "Come on, the morning will be here by the time you two get your arses in gear! Walker, drop if you have to, we can catch the girl after. Remember to bend the knees, or they will end up in your arse."

Daisy heard the little man laugh to himself below.

Walker let go of the railing and turned to her, "As he says then, girl. I'll go first and then y—"

Daisy cut him off by sliding though the railings, feet first. She hit the ground with a crunching scatter of gravel and bird bones, just managing to keep from tumbling forward. She stood and exhaled, slightly lightheaded.

Benny eyed her up, nodding. "Impressive, girl. Show him how it's done eh?" He chuckled and looked up. "Come now, old man, your turn." Benny turned away and busied himself with a rusted hatch on the roof top, as Daisy spoke to Walker.

"Come on Walker, it's not far. Jump."

Walker scowled down at her, "I will. When I'm ready."

He stood up, and she saw him take a deep breath and a step back. He then leapt the railing, landing heavily. Daisy heard the hissing of his boots and the popping in his armour as they took the brunt of the impact. Walker straightened up, brushing himself off, nodding to Daisy.

"How dramatic," Benny muttered, "Right, the gang's all here. Let's get out of this rain, shall we?"

He opened a hatchway with a light flourish, revealing a square patch of darker darkness, and another drop.

36

Walker scanned the tunnel they had arrived in. It ran underneath the warehouse building they had entered through the skylight earlier, and contained old containers and boxes, and not much light.

Benny was ahead of him, using one of his high-tech gadgets to check for heat signatures, lasers and all sorts of intruder detecting things Walker knew little about.

Daisy dropped with a light splash behind him, crouched and weapon drawn.

"You won't need that yet, girl. We have to be as quiet as possible."

Daisy looked up at him from behind her visor, "No problem." She slipped her gun back into its holster, "You have any other weapons for me then? Because that's all I have."

Walker looked back at her, thinking. He *could* use his body as a more effective weapon, but decided to keep the knife for himself.

"Find a rock." He replied.

She considered him for a moment, but nevertheless began to search around, checking the boxes and debris around them. She finally came up with a decent fist sized rock, and grimaced at him.

Benny had finished his scan, and turned to them, "Right, it's like a maze down here, but things seem quiet. Keep behind me, stay quieter than I do, and if I run, you should too."

Walker nodded, and began to follow the wiry man, Daisy falling into place behind him. He could hear her breath, short and fast. He turned to her as they darted along the darkened corridors below the city.

"Control your breathing, girl. Stay calm. We'll have the element of surprise down here, remember that."

She nodded, and hefted her rock. "And I have this, don't forget." She whispered, half joking.

They moved through the belly of the city, pausing irregularly to allow Benny to check, mutter and scan for problems. Walker soon lost all sense of where they were, despite his best efforts at memorising the route, for their escape later. He muttered his misgivings to Benny.

"Thief, how do the girl and I get out of this hole?"

Benny paused and goggled at him in the darkness, "How is that my problem, walker? You wanted to get into the Library. I'm helping. That was the deal."

Walker grabbed at the man's leather jacket as he turned away. Benny spun around, brandishing a twisted, evil looking knife. The slick edge glowed sickly yellow in the dull light thrown by the tunnel's ceiling lamps.

"Let go, boy, I ain't scared of you, like the others, and I'm tired of you bossin' me about, calling me thief an' that. I could leave you, down here in the gloom, to die all alone. But I won't; I like Charlie, so I'm doing him this favour. But once you're in there, you are alone. Apart from her," he motioned with his knife to Daisy. "Now, let go, and come on. It's going to be light out by the time we get there."

Walker glared at the man, but let him go. The knife slowly moved away, and made a slinking sound as it slid back into the man's hidden sheath. Benny watched Walker for a second more, then moved on again, faster through the shadows.

Walker spat, and followed. Daisy whispered from behind him, over the dull splashing of their boots in the wet. "Walker, he said he's going to leave us in there? How will we get out?"

Walker carried on in silence for a while, thinking. He had trusted that this man would stay, and wait for them to return, leading them back from the tunnels to the streets.

"Never mind, girl. We'll think of something." He pulled his hat lower down his face and moved on.

37

Daisy hefted the rock in her hand, as Benny fiddled with something on his wrist. She hadn't decided if Walker was joking or not when he told her to find the rock, but she felt it'd be better to have it and not need it, than need it and get stabbed in the murky dark of the tunnels.

Ahead of her Walker sat on his haunches, looking at the cigarette he had rolled. He placed it back into his pocket and looked to Benny, who was muttering.

"What is it?" He asked.

Benny half turned, still focused on whatever was causing him grief. "This thing is telling me that we've gone too far, but this one tells me we've not gone far enough." He tapped the square instrument on his wrist, and shook it.

"Fix it, man, we haven't got all day."

"Oh, now he gets a sense of urgency." Benny snorted. He turned back to his device and dragged over a half rotted crate. He placed the device on it, and started to undo the screws along its back panel. "This won't take long. Happens sometimes. It's the ground above us, blocks the signals."

Walker grunted and peered over the man's shoulder, pointing, and the two of them began to discuss what could be wrong with Benny' machine. Daisy was about to go over and watch, when she was overcome by a strange feeling of being watched.

She quickly turned her head towards the way they'd come, scanning for movement. She saw only water dripping, splashing quietly from the dank ceiling into the pools on the floor, sending ripples outward.

She glanced back at Walker, saw he was still arguing quietly, and decided to check the tunnel behind them. She unclipped her holster, despite what Walker had said about silence, and ventured out.

The lights above her buzzed uninterestedly, flickering occasionally. She could almost taste the slime coating the ancient brickwork. A lone drip landed on her head and ran down her neck, sending out chills through her body.

Her hackles rose as she inched forward, and her fingers answered by gripping the rock hard, until her knuckles shone white.

After what felt like an age, moving as slowly as she was, she reached the opening of the stretch of tunnel they were in, where it branched off to the left and the right.

She steeled herself and, rock ready, twisted from the corner and into the darkness.

There was nothing.

She quickly turned about, to face the second opening, and was relieved when she found nothing. She saw Walker looking back at her, head to one side. She stood straighter and waved an arm at him, to show everything was okay.

It was as she began to head towards the pair ahead of her, still fussing over Benny's various instruments, that she heard it.

The grating noise.

The chuckle.

She turned again, and the junkie removed himself from the shadows. He still wore his blue robes, but he was grimy with the dirt of the sewers. He had found another helmet, more streamlined, less bulbous. Wires protruded from the back, seemingly entering the junkie's head and neck. His mouth still leered from under the visor, which was now a deep crimson. He was smiling.

Daisy drew back the rock, ready, "What are you doing here?"

The man frightened her, but not because he was a threat. It was the way he seemed to have no grip on... anything. He stood there, teetering in the gloom, the flickering light behind her sending strange shadows dancing across his skeletal frame.

The figure nodded its head, indicating Walker and Benny, still focused solely on the tracking machines. "Still, the blind follow those who cannot see."

Daisy watched the strange figure before her. He seemed less twitchy now, but still made little sense. She wondered what was going on behind the crimson screen.

"Blind? None of us are blind. It's you who can't see. Why are you here?"

There was a rasping sigh and the helmet turned to her, "The lack of foresight, hindsight and insight is," he drew a sucking breath, "Tiring." He seemed to rattle as he exhaled. Daisy wasn't sure if he was laughing or dying, but she took a step back anyway.

"Just tell me why you're here, or I'll—" she waved the rock again.

This time the man did notice it, but he only smiled, bearing rank bluish gums at her, the odd tooth protruding like gravestones in mud. "But first she tells me why she is here, for me to have followed? Why are we all here? Finding what has been lost? Or losing what they've only just found?" He turned his head to her and stepped forward.

Daisy watched, warily, holding her ground. "Why should I tell you?"

The thing rattled again, "She doesn't know!"

He rubbed his hands together gleefully as Daisy bristled, "He's helping me. I'm helping him."

The helmet bobbed up and down, the neck below threatening to snap under the slight movement. "Help, help is good. But is he helping you? You don't even know why you are here."

Another suck of air, "How can there be help if there is nothing to help with?" He leaned forward, but Daisy wouldn't move back again. She wasn't afraid of this thing. The helmet twitched, and he grinned again. "The necklace. Skulls always smile."

Daisy clutched at her necklace, finally caving and moving back again.

This time, the apparition stayed where it was, skeletal grin playing in the dripping light. "Sentiment with a smile," another rattle.

Daisy was feeling less confident with each passing moment. The idea that this creature should know so much of the two of them, and of what she was thinking, frightened her. "Why do you wear that thing?" she asked him, indicating the helmet, "It's made you mad."

The man took a step backwards giggling, waggling a finger knowingly, "We're all mad here." He smiled that empty, knowing smile, and rattled a third time at her.

Daisy had had enough. Steeling herself, she darted forward and grabbed the man roughly by the front of his filthy tunic, ignoring the foulness of his breath. "Enough riddles, just get out of here." She pushed him roughly away, and he stumbled. "Before Walker sees you, and I have to do something."

She pocketed the rock and turned away, feeling disgusted. It wasn't just the man's smell or lack of hygiene, which was plentiful, but the way he spoke, the way he stood, his laugh, his laboured breathing and the dull, crimson bar blocking his eyes.

She found herself again wondering what had happened to this disgusting little man, what it was that had broken him so completely. She shivered.

She had begun to move back towards Walker and Benny, when the junkie whispered to her in a sing song voice, echoing slightly around her.

"I am lost, still not found, though now blind, still see, and though the world spins round and round, the key to this, is me."

Daisy stopped and spun back to him, causing the water around her sodden boots to splash against the wall. As Walker turned to see what had made the noise, Daisy looked into the shadows for the junkie, but he was gone.

She glowered into the darkness, hand resting on her pistol. She heard Walker carefully making his way up the tunnel behind her.

"What is it, girl?"

She noticed he had his knife ready, and his holster unclasped. Daisy continued to scour the dull, dripping murkiness ahead of her, but could see nothing.

"Girl?"

Daisy turned her head sharply, but let it go. "Nothing, Walker. Just a rat."

Walker's face remained passive as the visor stared at her. Finally he straightened up, and nodded. "Come on, then. Our guide knows the way. Finally."

He loped down the tunnel, leaving Daisy behind. She took one last look into the shadows and followed, the junkie's dying chuckle ringing in her ears.

Walker gazed at the heavy doorway, thinking. Benny had left them some time ago, refusing to actually go underneath the library itself, so Walker had left the rat to scurry away.

He rubbed his chin, taking in the door. It was large, set into the concrete wall of the tunnel ahead. Faded warning signs and peeling yellow paint plastered its rusted, blood red surface. It looked impregnable, and powered down.

Walker cursed inwardly, and crept forward. The tunnel here was darker; the lights had been removed, but it was at least dryer. There were no leaks in the library above; the Librarian wouldn't allow his books to be damaged.

"How are we going to open it?" Daisy asked, knelt at his side.

He ran a hand over the door, ignoring the control panel to the left. His visor was making up for the darkness, but he couldn't make all of it out. His fingers traced the bumps and gouges, bullet wounds and blast marks scoured the pitted metal surface, marking signs of some forgotten battle.

He felt along the bottom of the door, feeling for any gaps, a draft, any space he could get a hand in and try to lift. Nothing.

Walker cursed quietly and stood up.

Daisy spoke, "Walker, why don't—"

He silenced her with a wave, "Not know, girl. I'm thinking."

She frowned at him, "Don't start that again. Look, why don't we—"

He turned to her, "Look, there's no way in. The door is closed tight. We'll have to go back, find another route. Maybe we can catch up with the thief, see if he knows of another doorway."

Daisy shook her head as Walker turned from the door, rubbing his chin. It seemed that the roof top was the best way in, after all. The guards would be a problem, though, Walker thought to himself.

He started to make his way back down the tunnel, when he was brought out of his brooding by a single, low beep.

He turned to see Daisy, standing, arms folded, by the door's control panel, which was now emanating a soft, blue glow that pulsed slowly, bathing them intermittently in eerie half light.

"What did you do?" Walker asked.

Daisy tilted her head, visor flashing with the beat of the panel's light. "I just tried the button. To see if it would work."

Walker shook his head. He had assumed that the power was off in this area. "Press it again," he grunted.

Daisy obliged, and the pulse stopped, replaced by a solid glow. There was a low rumbling, and the door started to slide, edging its way slowly upwards. She half bowed, spreading her arms, "Tah-dah," she said, "Like magic."

Walker grunted at her, "Fair enough, don't get big headed about it."

Daisy smiled slightly, turning to watch the door's progress.

Walker was about to warn her about what may lay ahead, when there was a grinding noise, and the door halted. There was a metallic snap of metal, and the door shuddered, locking into place. The light on the control panel blinked, and went out

He sighed. "Damn."

The gap the door had left was too small for either of them to crawl through. He pressed the button again, but nothing happened.

He took his hat off and ran his hand through his hair. He was tired. He went to shift the bag on his shoulder, but his hand grasped at nothing. He gritted his teeth and turned to Daisy. "Get a hand on that door, girl."

She looked at him, flicking her visor up. "You're not going to try to lift it, surely? The thing must weigh a tonne"

She watched as Walker stretched, spreading his arms out across his chest. He rubbed his hands together, and flexed, stretching the leather of his gauntlets.

"He is..." Daisy shook her head. "Okay, what are we doing?"

Walker looked at her, "There should be another panel on the opposite side of the door. I need you to roll under and find it. Hopefully, it still works."

Daisy looked from him to the door, and back again. "Roll under that? What if it drops?"

Walker's face remained impassive, "It won't." He tapped his chest plate, making a dull ringing noise. "The rig will take most of the weight. Just be quick."

Daisy looked back to the door, and took a deep breath.

"Okay."

Walker clasped her shoulder, briefly, then took his position at the door. He stretched his back, one more time, then hunkered down. "Ready, girl?"

"Ready."

Walker grabbed the bottom of the door and tensed, waiting for the lifters on his back plate to notice and take up the strain. They began to hiss, his cue to lift. He began to straighten up, and the hissing grew. There was a crunch, a scream of metal, and the door began to shift, ever so slightly.

Walker gritted his teeth and tried to straighten further, but couldn't. The veins on his neck leapt out, and the rig took more of the strain. The lifters in his boots began to trill, and a warning tone pealed from his chest plate, signalling that he was attempting to lift too much. He ignored it.

The door shifted again, just an inch, and the hissing was replaced by a high pressure whine. Spots began to flash in Walker's vision as he heaved at the door.

He felt Daisy drop to the ground next to him, ready to roll through the gap. He shut his eyes, gathered his remaining strength, and pulled, willing the door to shift. It did, just.

He felt her brush past his leg as she tucked through the gap, "I'm through!"

He darted back as the door slammed. Walker dropped to one knee, breathing hard, trying to clear the dark patches from his vision. He retracted his visor and wiped the sweat from his eyes.

Walker made to stand, but fell backwards, landing heavily. The tone from his armour still rang, informing him that the rig was damaged. He flapped a hand wearily at a switch near his neck and silenced it.

He sat in the dust, lungs burning, ears straining for any sound from the other side of the door. How would he get in if Daisy couldn't find the switch, or got caught? He'd have to head to the roof anyway, after all that effort. He spat into the darkness and bowed his head.

39

Daisy had rolled through the gap, and was now trying to lie as still as possible. As she had entered, she had noticed an eye on the ceiling, watching the door. It whirred and clicked, a small red light blinking next to its darkened lens. The eye swivelled on a stick which ran in to the ceiling above it. Cables stretched out from its rear, also heading upwards.

The thing had turned, clicking rapidly at her, but had slowed when she remained still. She moved an arm experimentally. It continued to ignore her, until she waggled her arm quickly.

It swivelled and the clicking began anew, so she stopped. Right, she thought; if I move slowly, it ignores me.

She began to move, first painstakingly bringing her onto all fours, before slowly entering a low crouch. The eye remained focused at the door, red light blinking slowly. Daisy looked around her.

The eye was set in the corner of the chamber she had entered, to her right. Behind her was the door, this side better maintained and devoid of warning signs. Ahead and to her left, opposite the eye, was an opening, where she could see stairs heading upward; yellow light shone from somewhere ahead. The wall to her right was blank, solid grey concrete.

Daisy tucked herself into the corner behind her, bracing her back against the wall. There was a metal box, what Walker would have called a control panel, just above her. She strained her arm, careful to keep the eye uninterested. She groped, feeling for the button, until her fingers brushed its rounded surface.

The eye was sure to notice when she pressed the button, but there was nothing for it. She pressed, and the blue pulse started, with the soft tone she had heard earlier. To her surprise, the eye didn't swirl, but carried on staring at the door.

She held her breath and pressed again. The light turned solid, and the door began to grind. This time, however, the movement was sleek, and the door slid slowly upwards. The light on the eye blinked faster, and she heard the clicking.

She peered through the opening and saw Walker, hurriedly extending his visor. He began to speak, but Daisy shushed him.

She pointed to the corner, where the eye hung, clicking and blinking furiously.

Walker cursed. "It's a camera, they know we're here."

Daisy looked back at the camera, and felt the rock in her pocket. She stood and hefted it, launching it square at the camera. It struck the eye, cracking the black dome and sending it limp, still clicking.

"There," she said, pleased with herself, "It can't see us now."

Walker strode past her, towards the light, "Too late, girl. Come on, quickly."

He turned the corner and vanished, taking the stairs two at a time. Daisy began to follow, pausing only to look at the eye. The light was flashing furiously, and she could hear it trying desperately to turn and follow them.

Walker had paused, and looked down at her. "Girl, I'm giving you one last chance to leave, to go home, if you want."

Daisy looked at him. He stood there, dusty cloak limp behind him, mud spattered jeans faded in the yellow light. His face was dark under the hat, but she could see the grim line of his mouth.

"I told you at Charlie's; I've come too far now. *We've* come too far. I have nowhere to go, even if I wanted to."

He stood there for a moment, rubbing his chin. Finally, he nodded. He went to turn, but she spoke again.

"Just one more thing, Walker. I need you to tell me why you gave me that book, all those years ago. Was there some reason, some actual point?"

Walker turned fully towards her, considering her with his silver gaze, rasping his chin with a calloused thumb.

"You needed it."

She clenched her fists, annoyed, "Nothing else?"

He continued to regard her, scratching his stubble. He spoke. "I suppose you reminded me of someone I used to know."

"Okay," she exhaled, "And will we make it? Will you be able to get me into the Order? You are Walker, after all."

She tried a smile. Walker continued to look down at her. His cheek muscles rippled slightly, until he grinned.

"Of course. With the right knowledge, anything is possible."

Daisy nodded, still slightly unsure, and headed up the stairs, into the light.

40

11 years ago...

"What do you mean I have to go?" bellowed the boy.

Walker stood outside the bar, smoking quietly. "You heard me. You have to go. I've taught you all I can."

He looked at the boy, who could see himself, as always, reflected in the silver of his visor. Walker couldn't do this, he thought to himself. Train him up and then let him go, for what?

"I'm supposed to help fight the Order, join the Walkers, work with you! Walker, that was the whole point of... of all of this!"

Walker looked away, exhaling silver blue smoke in the twilight. "No, boy. I saw a lost little boy with nothing but a stick and a temper, and gave him a life, taught him how to live. I never said anything about you fighting with us."

The boy clenched his fists, teeth grinding, "And what will you do? Just go on running away, you and the other walkers, hiding in the shadows, leaving the Order to do as they please?"

Walker sighed, and his shoulders slumped. "I... have to go away too. Stop all of this. The Walkers, we..." He waved a weary hand at his satchel, which he had dropped on to the floor.

The boy stopped for a moment; Walker, giving up his books? It was unthinkable! The man had nothing else.

"What happened in there?" he asked, pointing accusingly to the smoky interior behind them.

Walker sighed, and flicked his cigarette away. "I met a friend. Michael, I told you about him. The man I trained with, at the academy.

"He told me the Order are on to us. They've been watching us for some time, and it's only him that has prevented them from picking us up and... doing whatever it is they do to walkers in the library."

"So what? We've always gone against the Order, it's what walkers do!"

It was Walker's turn to shout, "You are not a Walker, lad!" He softened when he saw the boy's face, and continued, "We have done what we can. The Walkers are a lost cause. We've already lost too many."

The boy growled at him, "What happened to you? You started all of this. The walkers followed you, did as you said. Now look at you," he hefted Walker's satchel, and threw it at his feet, "You're weak. That Walker, Idris, he was right. They should be following me."

Walker sighed again. "He's dead lad. Almost all of them are dead."

The boy continued to glare at him, jaw muscles tensing and rippling "Then we hit back, take revenge. Go out fighting, not whimpering!"

Walker shook his head. "No lad, I'm tired. Tired of all of this. I never should have left. We were wrong. Father was wrong."

The boy couldn't believe his ears. "So you're turning your back on everything you believed in, because you're old?"

He spat, "And what am I going to do? I have nothing now! What was the point? You should have left me in that town, all those years ago."

Walker stepped closer again to him, his face under the visor a mask of sadness. "Boy, forgive me. But it wasn't all to waste. You can take your skills back with you, go home and be a good, strong man in your town."

The boy was enraged again, "Go home? Go home? I'm hundreds of miles away, in some strange place, and you want me to go home? I don't even have a name!"

Walker wilted further, shoulders slumped. The thunder in the boy's ears rose, blocking out the wittering noise of the man who had been his master.

He didn't deserve to lead the Walkers. He stared furiously at the armour and the hat; symbols of the Order, and the silvery strip on the man's face; at the visor that blocked the wearer's eyes from view. The boy saw himself reflected there, for the thousandth time, and something snapped, slowly and painfully.

"...can help you get home. Here" Walker finished speaking, and held out his money bag. The boy took it, and looked at Walker numbly. "And now I have to go." He said sadly.

He hefted his battered satchel and headed down the west road, into the darkness of the woods.

The boy watched, thoughts racing as he rubbed his chin.

41

Daisy watched Walker as he stood ahead of her, picking a lock. She heard the pick rasping as it scraped around inside of the door, and cast her eyes about, wary of any guards. So far, they had met no one; no caretakers, no guards; no one. This worried her, and she knew it worried Walker more. He had expected a full on fire fight.

As they had headed upwards into the belly of the building, it had started to change, surprising her. From ancient dripping stonework, up through the barren, bare concrete of the lower levels, they had reached areas that could only be described as luxurious.

The corridors and staircases that wound through the building were grand, wide affairs, lined with doors marked with words Daisy did not recognise. Ancient portraiture lined most of the walls, depicting noble, imperious looking men and women, wearing clothes that seemed too billowy and complicated to be practical in any way. She saw teachers and generals, soldiers and queens. Great moustaches glared down at her, and angry eyes watched as they scuttled through the depths of the library.

Despite the nerves setting her stomach on edge, she was impressed; she had never been in such a place. Charlie's bar had seemed fairly posh, at least when compared to her local pub in her village, but this place, it was like a palace.

She turned back to Walker as the door clicked sullenly, and swung inwards.

Walker waved to her, and they crept forwards into the darkness, their boots padding gently on the carpeted floor. She could make out high backed dining chairs set around a long table that ran the length of the room; she could hear the rain attacking the windows to their left, but the view was blocked by heavy curtains.

Walker had stopped a few paces ahead at another door, which he tried. It wasn't locked, and creaked ajar at his touch. He froze, and hissed at her.

She slunk next to him and looked to where he was pointing. The hallway ahead of them glowed softly with the orange light of a lamp, which was sitting next to two enormous doors. They were wooden, polished to such a high shine that the glow from the lamp made them seem alight with fire; heavy iron banding gleamed oily dark against the doors, giving them an air of impenetrability.

Daisy's heart had leaped into her mouth. It was the library. The word was carved into the heavy stone set above the door in big, gothic lettering, but she could still make it out. Walker half turned to her, and motioned to his visor. Daisy nodded and flipped her visor down in response.

He nodded and they set off again, trying to avoid the pool of light oozing from the lamp. Walker braced up against the doors, slowly pressing his weight. They began to shift, silently brushing along the soft carpet. As the crack widened, Daisy ventured a look, over Walker's head.

The room ahead was vast. The far wall was almost all glass; she could see the stormy infancy of dawn beginning to break through the long elegant windows, flashes and crackles of lightning from the storm outside briefly illuminated the huge pillars and arches of the ceiling above. As the crack in the door widened, she could make out details; the walls of the room were angled together, to form a huge hexagon. All around the room, as far as she could see, were bookcases; narrow rows of them circled the raised platform, also hexagonal, in the middle of the room.

She could make out tables and chairs on the platform, with lamps and what looked like writing supplies on them. In the centre of the chairs was a large dais, which rose imperiously from the stone platform.

She stood there mouth agape, taking it all in. Walker finished opening the heavy doors and stood next to her. She turned to ask him a question, when she noticed his mouth open. "What is it?" she asked immediately, readying her pistol, thinking he had seen something.

"It's so... big." He managed.

Daisy looked up at him questioningly; he had been acting strangely ever since they had escaped the concrete underbelly below them. She had expected him to know his way around the building, but they had back tracked and ended in dead ends more times than she cared to think of. Now he was reacting like this to a room he should be more than familiar with?

"You *have* been here before, right?"

He turned to her and closed his mouth hurriedly, setting it in its familiar grimace. "Of course I have, I... just..." he cleared his throat. " It's been a while. Come on, maybe he left the books in here. Either way, we're in the right place."

He sloped carefully forward, making his way around the old, stone librarian's desk in front of the doors. She followed suit, taking care to stay close to the bookcase to her right. She glanced quickly at the tomes and works as she passed. There were too many titles to take in; there must be thousands of books on this side of the case alone.

Walker paused at the end of the case, and glanced about him, taking care to scan the shadows between the looming shelves around them. Daisy looked about her as well, taking in the high domed ceiling, shadowy and dark way above them.

They reached the edge of the raised platform, and began to climb. Walker stalked ahead, pistol drawn and loose at his side, his shoulders hunched in the gloom. He stopped at the top, and rested his hands on the podium. Daisy stood next to him, still scanning the room for anything that might be skulking in the darkness.

The top of the podium was flat, a smooth piece of glass that bathed Walker's face in soft, blue light when he tapped on it with a finger. A pleasant tolling noise rang out, causing Daisy to flinch. Walker waved a hand in her direction and returned his gaze to the screen. Despite herself, she peered over his shoulder, watching. He was scrolling through lists, the words speeding past too quickly for her to read any of them.

There was a crunch, bringing them out of their search. Walker looked up quickly, pointing his pistol into the darkness ahead of them. Daisy stared intently, but could make nothing out. A calm, sombre voice called out from the shelves.

"That's enough of that, Walker. It's time for you to leave. Take the girl and go, one last time."

Walker gritted his teeth, "I'm here for the books you took, Librarian."

She could just make out a shadow amongst the darkened shelves ahead, getting closer. The man stepped out and stood looking up at them. He was tall and slim, dressed like Walker, but all in black, and far smarter. His armour was polished and gleamed darkly, and his hat was tall and dark. His visor was nearly jet black, and it came down over his nose. She could faintly make out the sad smile from below.

"It's him!" Daisy growled.

Walker didn't turn, but murmured down to her, "Don't move, girl; he has men watching us."

Daisy froze, her hand trembling. This was the man who had had her father beaten to within an inch of his life, and had taken their treasure.

He spoke again, heading slowly towards them. "Yes, Walker is right girl, don't do anything rash. We can all walk away from this."

He waved a gloved hand and soldiers appeared from between the rows of bookcases around them. Their rifles were trained on Walker and Daisy, and they whirred slightly in the dusty quiet.

"Put those away, the two of you. We should talk first."

Walker turned his head slightly to Daisy, then nodded. They holstered their guns, and the Librarian began his ascent towards the dais. He reached it, and scrolled in the same manner Walker had been.

"What are you doing here now, Walker? You know what I said last time. You know what Mother thinks of you."

He glanced at Walker, then resumed his scrolling.

"I'm afraid your books are in processing. Quite a sad little bundle, really. Stories and cookbooks." He shrugged, "Still. Valuable in their own way. They're better off here," he added as Walker tensed, "This way, they will last forever."

124

"They were mine, Librarian." Walker grunted.

The Librarian tilted his head slightly at him, "Always so formal, Richard?"

Walker flinched. The Librarian shrugged again, and stepped away from the dais. "Either way, what you were searching for isn't on the list. It's in my personal collection; hidden away."

Daisy looked up at Walker, who was staring at the Librarian with hatred, his lips thin and pale.

The Librarian began again, "Still taking on apprentices I see? We discussed this Walker."

He rounded on the girl, leaning in close, "Why are you here, girl? Hoping for entry to the Order? Entranced by the tale of the noble walkers?"

Daisy opened her mouth to reply, but her cut her off.

"You aren't the first," he straightened up, "There was a boy, once."

Walker flinched again. Daisy raised an eyebrow at him, but spoke to the Librarian, "I'm here with Walker. We've come for his books."

The Librarian smiled his sad smile at her. "That's not all your Walker has come for. He wishes to change things. Become one with the Order again," He turned to Walker, his smile even sadder, "Which he knows is impossible, for reasons we need not discuss here."

He walked back to the dais, and flicked a gloved finger across it. The screen flashed, and the merry tinkling noise played again, and the dais went dark.

"Come Walker, leave. Mother is already... upset with me for leaving you be so long. Take this girl and go. Stop this foolishness. It's only a matter of time before she dies too."

Daisy clenched her fists. No one would use her name. It was bad when Walker did it, even worse when this man, the man that had caused her family to die, did it too.

She spoke up, no longer able to contain herself. "Why can't we change things? Walker said that knowledge is power. Why couldn't we kill you, all of you, and make things right?"

Walker half turned to her, as did the Librarian. His smile was gone, his mouth a slim line.

"What Walker has planned, what you might have planned, it wouldn't work. Changing a book, whilst being inhumanly criminal, is also not a valid way of changing history. It would take more than scrawling childishly on ancient tomes to change what has happened. Go home."

She noticed Walker flinch for a third time, as the Librarian began to head back down the steps. "My men will escort you out, and you will leave. Try Europe. It's largely unaffected by the weather these days. You can't stay here, though, you clearly can't be trusted."

There was a click to her left, as Walker raised his pistol. Daisy watched, heart thudding in her chest, as he trained it on the Librarian's back.

"He said we could change history. He said whoever has the power, the knowledge, can change what they like, what they need."

Walker's voice sounded different. It scared Daisy; normally his voice teetered between the gravelly mocking and the surly growling that she had gotten used to, but this sounded... different.

More animal.

More desperate.

The Librarian stopped and turned, slowly. The soldiers below them continued to point their rifles; blue targeting lights flicked on, bathing them in an icy stare. Daisy heard faint voices coming from the soldiers; pleasant and calm sounding voices relaying information.

The Librarian spoke, peering up at Walker, "He? Who is 'he', Richard? Of whom do you speak?" He shook his head, "Something has happened to you, old friend. You've changed. Leave, now. Before I change my mind."

He turned again and made his way towards his soldiers.

Daisy watched Walker; his jaw muscles rippling under his skin, his hands clenching and unclenching. "Walker? Come on, what are we going to do?" She was furious herself; that man had caused so much pain.

Walker said nothing.

Daisy glared up at him from behind her silvery visor, "Fine!" she shouted, dashing forward. "If you won't do something, I will!"

She raised her heavy pistol, flicking the switch on the grip. The machine started to squeak and whir as the overcharge built up inside it. The Librarian turned, his own heavy pistol raised squarely at her.

Time seemed to slow.

She saw the soldiers moving, rifles swinging from Walker to her, she felt Walker grab at her arm as he twisted next to her.

She saw the flash of the Librarian's gun, the flame bursting savagely from the barrel.

She heard the boom the round made as it left its chamber.

She felt her necklace, with her brother's tag on it, cold against her chest, as the slug ripped through her chest.

She tasted the metal tang of blood on her tongue.

She felt the air leave her lungs, and the ice that replaced it.

She felt herself die.

126

42

Walker caught Daisy as she fell, ducking the salvo of rifle fire that came their way. He bounded down the stairs, three at a time, towards the stone receptionist post near the doors. They skidded into cover, and he laid her gently down onto the carpeted ground.

He had no time to check on her: the soldiers were moving closer, he could hear their headsets crackling, tinny voices relaying information. He set himself and stood, quickly. He spun his arm around, sighting along his pistol. He fired off six quick rounds; the two nearest gunmen dropped, bodies dropping awkwardly on each other before tumbling down the stairs.

There were six men left, and the soldiers returned in kind. Blue flashes roared vengefully from their rifles, sending angry hornets buzzing towards him. He dove sideways, rolling and springing towards one of the stone columns supporting the arched ceiling far above him. He felt the jolts as the rounds slammed into the stone behind him. He grunted and released the chamber on his gun. The spent rounds fell out, and he replaced them quickly, sliding them in and spinning the housing.

He slipped from his position and headed left, firing up at the soldiers on the platform. Blue flashes illuminated the room; deep shadows danced and leapt about on the walls around them.

Walker heard the Librarian shouting.

"Don't damage the shelves! Some of those books are the last of their kind!"

Walker ducked between two of the shelves, shredded paper falling around him as the soldiers ignored the order. He heard the crack of the philosopher's magnum, but no rounds came his way. He peered around the case for a quick glance towards his attackers. The soldiers had fallen back, and two more lay dead. He had fired on his own men.

Walker hid again, and made his way quietly down another isle. He heard the Bookmen's boots slamming on the marble as they regrouped.

"Walker." The Librarian called. "Why are you doing this? You know we can't allow this to happen!"

Walker reached the end of the bookcases and counted from three. On one, he stepped around the corner into the isle, arm outstretched. The soldier was not quick enough. Walker grabbed the man's rifle and pulled, hard. The strap holding his gun pulled him down, into Walker's rapidly raising knee. As the man doubled up, Walker slammed his elbow into the joint between the man's helmet and back plate. He heard a crack, and Walker threw the body from him.

More soldiers appeared at the opening in the bookcases and Walker heard the honeyed feminine voices crackling from their weapons confirm the target; he ducked quickly down the next isle, just dodging the salvo.

The Librarian called again forlornly, "Walker. You're trapped now. Obviously it pains me to allow my men to fire near the books, but this cannot continue."

Walker could hear the soldiers creeping slowly towards either end of the isle he had taken refuge in.

He shouted, to give his position away, "You're wrong about the records, Librarian. I'll change them, and get Walker back in to the Order."

There was no reply. Walker couldn't hear the soldier's boots anymore either. This was a good sign.

As the first man spun around the corner, the book Walker had thrown smashed into his visor, cracking the screen and knocking him backwards into the Bookman behind him. Walker twisted his body towards the attacker at the other end of the isle behind him, bringing his pistol to level.

Exhaling gently, he fired two rounds in quick succession. They both slammed into the soldier's chest plate. The man staggered, firing randomly. Walker ducked, grunting in pain. One of the bullets had grazed his arm, but he had no time to focus on it.

He was sprinting back towards the first attacker, whose partner had stepped over his writhing friend. As the man raised his rifle Walker dived, launching himself full bodied into him. The men tumbled, rolling and grappling, crashing into a bookcase and sending papers and books crashing down. The soldier was well trained; he had managed to come out on top of Walker and had immediately discarded his rifle and gone for the knife at his hip. But Walker was ready with the old knife he had taken from the veteran, days before.

"Shi—"

Walker stabbed, twice, killing the man quickly. He rolled the dead man off of him and stood up. The Bookman with the cracked visor had crawled away, leaving his weapon, and the man at the other end of the isle wasn't moving. They could wait.

"Michael!" Walker boomed. His voice echoed around the cavernous library, bouncing from the huge stone pillars and high vaulted ceiling. The only answer was his own, angry voice.

Walker grunted, holding his arm. He made his way out of the isles, towards the centre of the room. He passed the stone reception booth, passed Daisy. He threw his head back, and roared.

"Michael! Bring me the book!"

Again, his own voice roared back at him, sounding lost and empty in the cavernous chamber.

He staggered up the stone stair to the reading platform, with the dais. He moved slowly to the centre of the raised platform and stopped. He was breathing hard, and tired. He looked about him. The bookcases spiralled outwards around the room, and ascended up into the darkened reaches above him.

"Michael?" His voice came back, tarred by the gloom and dusty with age. He looked around again. The room seemed empty. The bodies of the soldiers lay forgotten behind him, amongst fallen books and pages.

There was a faint rustle, and Walker sighed.

"Drop the weapon, Walker."

Walker did as he was told, his gun clattering to the floor. As it hit the stone, he spun and ducked, kicking out viciously. The Librarian merely stepped backwards, keeping his pistol trained on Walker.

Walker turned the kick into a leap, and sprang upwards. Michael sidestepped, slapping him aside easily. Walker snarled and turned, using his momentum and bringing his arm arching around, but the Librarian stepped forwards smartly, jabbing gently at his throat with a finger.

Walker crumpled, choking for breath. The Librarian looked down at him morosely and shook his head. His cloak flapped gently around him, caught in some unknown breeze.

"Too much brute strength, not enough thought, Walker. That is most unlike you."

Walker coughed, spitting blood. He began to crawl towards his pistol, but was turned on to his back by the Librarian's boot.

The Librarian peered down at him, frowning. "You look terrible, old friend."

Walker spat. "We... aren't..."

Michael smiled, sadly. "Yes, I know. I know." He stepped back and walked over to Walker's pistol. He picked it up, neatly tucking it into his belt.

He turned back, "Let's talk, Walker. So, what are you here for? Your books?" He gestured vaguely to the shelves spreading away from them. "They're already gone. Where they belong; safe, in my Library."

He began to pace around Walker, who still lay on the ground, gasping for air. "Or, was that just a cover for that silly old quest to get back into the Order?"

He held his arms out wide, as Walker rolled onto his side, wheezing. "You think, after all this, all that you've *done* over the years, that even *if* that book could help you to 'change history', that you'd be allowed back in?"

He shook his head again, and stood facing Walker as he climbed shakily to his feet. "What happened to you, Walker?"

Walker looked up at him. "What... do you mean?"

Michael continued to smile. "You've become unrecognisable, Richard. What happened to the young man I grew up with?"

Walker's left hand flinched at the name.

Michael's smile faded and he sighed again. "I fear that you won't stop, Walker. You'll keep going until we kill you."

He removed something from the satchel at his hip, and held it out to Walker. It was a book, thick and tattered. It had once been covered with some beautiful illuminations, but time had made it rough and dull.

"I have no desire to kill you, Richard. Here. Take it. Hopefully you'll learn from it. Try and change it, if you please. It's the history of the Order. We're in it. You, and I, Mother and Father. It talks about your little rebellion. We have other copies."

Walker eyed him and slowly took the booklet. He read the front. The title confirmed what the Librarian had said. It was indeed a history of the Order.

"He... once, he told me that whoever controlled these," he waved the book, feebly, "could control anything. Change things."

Michael watched, eyebrow raised, as Walker walked wearily away, down the stairs. "He? Who are you talking about? And what did you think would happen Dick? Richard?"

Walker stopped, but didn't turn back. "Stop calling me that." Walker said, voice weary and grey. "I can still change things, get in to the Order... Get the Walkers back... finish..." He trailed off and continued making his way down the stairs.

Michael paused, perplexed, but carried on. "Walker, you know what happened. You rebelled against Mother. We all blame Father for what happened to you, but you went too far. When Mother tried to bring back the old ways, the good ways... Father taught madness, and violence; he used knowledge for his own ends, to hurt people. Mother wishes to collect knowledge, redistribute it. People will learn again, Walker. What did *you* want from this?"

Walker ignored the accusing finger, "We wanted knowledge. Your Order tells lies, Librarian. He never told me any of that."

Michael cocked his head quizzically. "We? He? You didn't know what you wanted, you were just a child. *We* were just children." He sighed again, "And in light of that, of our friendship, I would rather not have to kill you. But I am the Librarian, and this is my library. And you will never, ever, be allowed to join us again."

Walker didn't respond. He continued down the stairs, slowly, heading for the heavy doors at the front of the hall.

"Do you know why Mother allows that you live?" Michael called from the top of the stairs.

Walker stopped and half turned, looking up at Michael.

130

"It's not that she feels badly for you. She does, but that's not it. It's not pity, nor selfishness, nor even cruelty. She knows you, Richard. She knows there is some good in you. But you cannot come back to us. She is waiting for you to go out in to the world, and undo some of the damage your walkers have caused. You could be a good man, Walker. She always said that."

Walker turned fully, facing Michael, looking up at him. He was everything Walker should have been. They had been together at the academy. Trained together as boys. Walker had been thrown out after his instructor had died.

"She doesn't know what kind of man I am."

Michael shook his head disapprovingly. "Of course she does, Walker. She took us in. Cared for us. Schooled is in the best possible manner. We learned the value of learning, and knowledge, and proper thought. We were to undo the wrongs of Father's madness. You were the favourite, Richard."

He sighed again and stepped lightly down towards Walker, stopping on the step above. "Richard. You must leave. If you take the girl now, she might live."

Walker sneered at him. "The girl is dead, Librarian. You are as bad a shot as I was told."

"Then, I am sorry. I will see that she gets a good burial."

Walker shrugged. "She's dead. I doubt she cares."

"I am sorry, Richard," Walker twitched at the repeated use of the name. "Truly I am. You could have been a good man."

Walker flinched again, but turned and started down the stairs. The Librarian grabbed his shoulder lightly. "I wish I knew where this insane idea had come from. So much harm could have been avoided."

Walker twitched again.

"Richard—"

Walker spun and grabbed Michael' arm, twisting it violently.

"Walker," he spat.

He plunged the veteran's knife into The Librarian's neck. Michael grunted in pain and fell, holding tightly to Walker and groping blindly for his pistol. Walker tried to get clear, but Michael' grip had become vicelike; he couldn't shake him.

They tumbled down the stairs. Michael had managed to free the knife, but was bleeding furiously. He fired at Walker; he felt the slug rip through him and he bellowed in pain. He swung his arm and battered Michael's pistol from his hand, before wrenching his own from Michael' belt.

The Librarian had knocked Walker's visor from his head, and now looked into his eyes. "Blue? But... You... you're not..."

Walker stood back, panting; his left leg could barely support his weight, but he couldn't feel it over the adrenaline. Michael lay before him gasping weakly. His visor had also been knocked from his face in the fall, and Walker could see the man's eyes. They were locked on his. He saw no anger, nor hatred, nor even sadness there, but simple confusion. He opened and closed his mouth, trying to voice questions, but no breath would come. His eyes glazed over, puzzled, as the life slowly left his body.

Walker lowered his pistol and stood there for a moment. Then, with shaking hands, he carefully reached into the pocket sewn into his cloak and, after wiping the blood from his hands, began to roll a cigarette.

He limped down the stairs, leaving the Librarian sprawled behind him, and retrieved his visor, clipping it together at the back of his head. He collected his hat from where it had fallen, and made his way to where Daisy lay.

He lit his cigarette, inhaling deeply, savouring the flavour. One day, these things were liable to kill him.

With some difficulty he knelt down. The hole in his leg was oozing blood, but he'd gotten lucky; the round had grazed his leg. Two close calls in one day. Lucky.

Daisy had not been so lucky.

He looked down at her body, limp in the weak morning sun pouring in from above. He checked her pulse, mainly from habit, and looked at her. Her wide, brown eyes stared unseeing upwards, and blood had trickled down her chin.

He gently closed her mouth, and her eyes, and sighed. As he went to stand, something yellow and silver caught his eye. It was the smiley face emblem; her brother's. He scratched his chin, then carefully removed the loop of leather from around Daisy's neck.

He stood up, cursing softly at the pain. He tore a strip from his cloak and tied it around his leg, for the bleeding, and looked around him. He took another drag on his cigarette.

He retracted his visor and bent to pick up the history book, which had fallen during the fight. He flicked through until he found Walker's page again, and stood in the dusty silence staring at it. Changing it would accomplish nothing, he thought bitterly.

After a while, he dropped it to the floor.

A few seconds later, the smiling necklace dropped too, landing face down on the stone.

And then Walker walked.

He always walked.

It was what he did.

EPILOGUE

10 years ago...

The boy lowered his pistol, flicking the empty rounds from the chamber, before sliding it into its holster. He grabbed the hat, removing it carefully from the corpse at his feet. He donned the hat and, after a second's thought, retrieved the visor from the ground. He looked at himself in its shiny surface and licked his lips.

The hat suited him perfectly, but there was something else... ah.

He knelt in the morning dew and began to work, removing the armour rig from its previous owner. He struggled it on; it was too big, and he had no idea how it worked. He played with a few switches here and there, finally managing to activate the hydraulic lifting plate, now on *his* back. There was a soft pealing tone, as the armour adjusted to his frame.

He examined himself in the visor again. Yes. He looked the part. He felt right. A walker. He lifted the book satchel onto his back, feeling the weight of it. He smiled easily to himself.

The leather cloak comes too, he decided; Walker had always worn it, it was part of the costume... no, not costume. Uniform. Official.

He nodded slightly, the outfit felt powerful, felt right, like something he'd been destined for. He'd never had a uniform before. Or power, come to think of it.

He draped the cloak about him, and patted down the pockets. There. The tobacco pouch. He grinned to himself and rolled a cigarette.

He patted the book satchel, its valuable contents now his to guard, and looked down at the body huddled at his feet.

"Sorry, old man, but you didn't deserve this. Walker should be someone people know, and fear."

The deep brown eyes stared accusingly up at him, unseeing and murky in the lightless dawn, the hard lines still etching a frown on Walker's face.

"I'll finish what you started."

He smiled to himself.

The boy finally had a name.

Walker.

13108005R00080

Printed in Great Britain
by Amazon.co.uk, Ltd.,
Marston Gate.